Shifter Chronicles

HIDDEN HYENA

CRISSY SMITH

Hidden Hyena
ISBN # 978-1-78686-355-3
©Copyright Crissy Smith 2018
Cover Art by Cora Graphics ©Copyright May 2018
Interior text design by Claire Siemaszkiewicz
Totally Bound Publishing

HIDDEN HYENA

Dedication

Thank you so much for joining me for the final book in the Shifter Chronicles series. The Coalition agents and other characters have been some of the funniest to write. There was a lot that went into this series and I know I wouldn't have been able to do it without having such an awesome editor. She manages to keep me focused and loves our men and women as much I do. Thank you, Rebecca, for everything.

Chapter One

The flashing blue and red lights illuminated the inside of the dirty, rundown convenience store. With blood coating his hands, Trent screamed into the radio for backup. Adam had gone so pale – Trent knew that wasn't a good sign.

"Please," he begged. "Please hurry." Where the hell is everyone? The other police officers should be here by now. "Where are you? Officer down! Officer down!" Trent shouted into the radio.

"Trent!"

Trent shot up in bed and gripped the arm of the person who'd been shaking him. "Mac?" His boss and best friend sat on his bed next to him.

"You were dreaming," Mac said.

"Screaming, you mean." Trent rubbed his hands over his face. The same nightmare, or memory, haunted him. The night Adam had died had been the worst of Trent's life. It didn't help that he kept reliving it.

"You want to talk about it?" Mac asked. He kept his voice quiet but had let go of Trent's arms. Mac already knew what had happened all those years ago. He was the only one Trent had told once he'd arrived in Brookside. Mac also knew Trent didn't like to be touched and Trent breathed easier when Mac stood, then took several steps away.

"No." Trent didn't want to talk. Or think.

"Okay, man," Mac said. "I'm going back to bed."

Trent waited until Mac had his hand on the door. "Mac."

Mac glanced over his shoulder.

"Thanks."

"I'm here for you," Mac responded. "Anytime."

All Trent could do was nod. He wished he could give in and be the man Mac wanted him to be. Mac believed the best of everyone who lived in the old bar and had become part of the family. But Trent wasn't ever going to open up like the others. He'd been betrayed too many times in his life.

Knowing he wouldn't be going back to sleep, Trent threw the covers off before climbing out of bed. He was already wearing a pair of sleep pants, so he grabbed his T-shirt off the top of the dresser and pulled it on before leaving his bedroom. The entire back area of The Den, a small bar in Brookside, California, had been made into small residences. Most of the shifters who lived there had done so for many years. They were the few people Trent considered his family.

He glanced at his watch. After four in the morning. The bar had been closed for a couple of hours, so everyone else should be in their rooms. Probably sleeping with no problems. Some of them would even be cuddled up to their lovers. *I'm not jealous, I'm not,* he told himself. It wasn't like Trent would ever have anyone to warm his bed for more than a few hours at a time. Good thing he worked in a bar. Plenty of opportunity to meet a woman, have sex and send her on her way. Trent was always up-front about what he wanted, so the females he slept with didn't give him trouble. A few showed up at the bar again, wanting him to take them to bed for another round, but Trent never slept with the same woman twice. He couldn't allow emotions to get involved. Luckily, most of the bed partners he picked understood the score.

Trent left the lights off as he made his way to the kitchen. He knew this place and while his shifter senses might not allow him to see in the dark, there were a few windows letting in enough light for his heightened eyesight to see.

Once in the kitchen, he turned on the small light above the sink so he could find his secret stash. Annabelle Sanchez, one of his favorite people in the world, always did a little shopping for the rest of them. Kelly, their cook, refused to allow them to eat anything processed or premade. But sometimes that was what they craved.

Opening the bottom cabinet, he reached back until his fingers brushed the top of a jar.

"Yes!" he hissed. Kelly sometimes found their stash and tossed the items. Not this time. Trent pulled out the jar of peanut butter. Kelly made an awesome strawberry jam which already had Trent's mouth watering thinking about it.

He made a peanut butter and jelly sandwich before cleaning up his mess. He did not want Kelly to find out he'd made himself a late-night snack. He'd never hear the end of it. Trent grabbed a beer before strolling out of the kitchen.

The back door led him to the quiet spot where Trent spent a lot of time.

He sat down at the picnic table and let the night settle around him.

Trent loved it out here. No one bothered him and he could stay for hours and hours. He loved to watch the sway of the tree limbs. The animals making a home inside the National Forest bordering their town would sometimes venture as far out as the bar.

In the shifter world, Trent's animal the lowest of the low. A hyena shifter was a joke to the other more popular species. To humans, Trent was a monster, an abomination. He'd never fitted in with anyone, not until he'd found a home at The Den.

But the natural animals that ventured this far reacted to Trent as if he were a predator. True, in his shifted form he had some crazy instincts, but he always had complete control of his animal side.

He ate his food while downing the rest of his beer. The others wouldn't be awake for at least six more hours. Just him and little critters he could hear skittering around. He needed to avoid thinking about the dream.

Adam had been his best friend since the day they'd been partnered together. Even after Trent came out to the public as a shifter, Adam's loyalty had never wavered. Too bad he couldn't say the same about his other friends or his lover. No one else had stood with him. And what had Adam gained by giving Trent that devotion? His death.

* * * *

Brookside, California. Melissa Bishop pulled her 2010 Titan truck up in front of the sheriff's office. She peered through her windshield at the old brick building. The blinds were open, so she could see the activity going on inside. Or a lack of activity.

There was a deputy sitting at a desk, but she couldn't see anyone else. It was still early. Just shy of seven o'clock in the morning. She wasn't due to report for her first day until eight, but Melissa had been anxious to begin her new life.

It had taken years and a lot of sacrifices to finally reach this stage in her career.

Melissa glanced at her hands. She was shaking. *Fuck, I need to get control of myself.* This was what she'd wanted. What she needed. The Shifter Coalition now worked side-by-side with the Brookside Sheriff Department. Melissa's chance to make amends started here. *Working side-by-side with shifters.*

Time to get started.

She pushed open her door, then leaned over and picked up her messenger bag. She stood and adjusted her khaki uniform. It was restricting and different. After the years of wearing the dark blue colors of the Los Angeles Police Department, she wanted this fresh start to work.

"Deputy Bishop."

Melissa spun around at the sound of the sheriff's voice. They'd only spoken on the phone, but she'd recognize the sound anywhere. "Sheriff."

Sheriff Magnus stood in the street, along with another man. They both held Styrofoam cups from the only coffee shop in town — Melissa had researched all the businesses around her new home.

Sheriff Magnus was a big guy, exactly as she'd pictured. The Brookside website reported him to be a tiger shifter. He'd been in charge of the Brookside Sheriff Department for three decades already. There wasn't a lot of information to be found on Magnus other than the website. He didn't even have a Facebook or Twitter account. She'd wanted to know her boss before taking the job, but he apparently didn't like posting pictures of his food.

The stranger wasn't as big as Magnus, but would still stand out in a crowd. Melissa had no idea how to tell what shifter species anyone might be. She didn't know if there was a secret to figuring it out or not. Hopefully she'd learn.

"You're here early," Magnus said.

"Anxious to get started," she replied.

"Fine." Magnus motioned with his cup to the other man. "This is Agent Logan Coldwell with the Shifter Coalition. I explained over the phone that we split an office with the Coalition."

"Yes, sir." Melissa turned to Agent Coldwell. "It's nice to meet you." He appeared to be pretty strait-laced. He wore a perfectly pressed blue suit.

"You, as well," Coldwell said.

"Well, let's go in. There's plenty of work to do," Magnus said.

"You're just mad because you have to meet with the park rangers today." Coldwell bumped Magnus as he started walking toward the office.

"Fucking assholes," Magnus spat.

Coldwell laughed. "I'll be there to make sure you don't kill them."

Magnus stomped forward, so Melissa hurried to follow along. She knew she had a lot to learn about working with shifters. She got the feeling these two men could fill in the missing pieces she sought.

Inside, the structure housing the Brookside Sheriff Department and the Shifter Coalition was disappointing. Instead of the large chrome-metal multi-floor office she was used to, her current job had her in a tiny building with crumbling concrete walls.

"Uh..." Melissa managed.

Agent Coldwell started laughing. "I told you it's ugly in here."

Magnus grunted. The fresh-faced young agent she'd spotted through the window glanced up and smiled.

"No, sir. No," she said. "It's…"

"Ugly," Coldwell repeated.

"It's a building that keeps the rain off our heads and allows us to do our jobs," Magnus stated.

"Yes, sir," she replied right away.

"Jesus," Magnus said. "Stop siring me to death. Call me Magnus."

Melissa stared at her boss. She'd never been allowed to call her superiors anything except their rank or sir. "Yes, s… Magnus."

"Good." He pointed to two desks covered in paperwork, where the lone deputy sat. "Those are taken." He motioned by the wall. "Take one of those. Drop your stuff off then come into my office."

"Yes, sir."

Magnus frowned at her.

"I mean Magnus."

He turned and stomped off to one of the two offices with glass doors and windows. Agent Coldwell had gone into the other office. Melissa strolled over where two desks were butted up against the other. Only a computer, monitor and mouse sat on each. Melissa set her bag down on the desk facing the door but put the offices behind her back.

Then she headed to her boss's office. She knocked on the doorjamb.

"Come in." Magnus lifted his head. "Sit."

He only had one chair in front of his large wood desk and she took it, then shifted around, trying to get comfortable.

"It's the worst chair I could find. Keeps people from coming in here just to blab."

"No blabbing, sir. I got it," she replied.

Magnus smirked. He pointed. "See that board?"

A white erase board hung on one wall of the sheriff's office. It was filled with numbers, a list of names, dates and status. "Yes."

"It's the reports of illegal hunting in the area in the last three months."

Melissa gaped at the board. "Only three months?"

"Each month there are more and more instances. This isn't only about hunting. There is some sort of conspiracy happening."

"That's why you're meeting with the park rangers," she hazarded a guess.

"Yes, although I don't believe it will do any good," Magnus said. "They don't want to get involved. They just tell me this is an issue a few fines can be given for."

"So you hired two more deputies."

"And pressured the Coalition to put agents in town," Magnus stated.

Melissa glanced over at the other office. Agent Colwell was on the phone while working on a laptop. His office, unlike the sheriff's, was filled with filing cabinets, boxes and clutter.

"You made waves in the LAPD," Magnus said.

Melissa sat up straighter. "Some would say."

"Everyone I spoke to said," Magnus responded.

"I pissed some people off." She looked her new boss in the eye. "And I don't regret it."

"So, tell me why," he ordered.

"I'm sorry?"

"There was something, some situation, which led you to the path you're on. I want to know what it is. And don't bullshit me."

"And if it's personal?" Melissa got the impression Magnus wouldn't give a damn.

"I don't care," Magnus said. "When I put the word out I was looking for two deputies, I received over forty applications. More than two-thirds were shifters."

"But you hired a human," Melissa said. She'd had no idea the competition had been so fierce.

"The other deputy starting this week is a shifter," Magnus said. "You are the only human who will be in this building. Will that be a problem?"

"No, sir," she replied.

"I'm taking a chance, allowing a human to protect an entire town full of shifters," Magnus said. "I did it because you made waves. Now, tell me why you did it. Why you applied with me for a position in this town in the middle of nowhere."

Melissa pressed her hands together. She already had the job. Magnus just wanted to know her story. Everyone had one, after all. She hated being in this position. Not that she blamed her boss—she was surprised Magnus hadn't asked her before. Melissa had thought carefully about her words and what she'd say.

"Have you ever heard of Detective Adam Cross?" she asked.

"No." Magnus leaned forward.

"He was a detective with the LAPD who worked in the gang unit. I'd recently been transferred to the missing persons division, but I knew him socially. He was killed one night after he and his partner stumbled onto a burglary at a local all-night store."

"A shifter?" Magnus had tightened his hand into a fist.

"Not him," she said. "His partner was, though. Adam could have asked for a transfer. It was common back then when the shifters...you announced your presence.

If a human wanted a different partner, the request would be granted."

"I've heard some stories about LAPD," Magnus said.

"The worst ones are probably true."

"But Adam stood by his partner," Magnus stated.

"He did. It made him unpopular."

"But I bet it was even harder for the shifter," Magnus said.

Melissa dropped her gaze to her hands. Her heart hurt. "Yeah," she said softly.

"So, this cop gets killed and…"

"They walked in on a burglary and the guy panics. He shoots Adam and the partner returned fire. Perp is dead, but Adam is bleeding out."

"Jesus," Magnus said.

"Adam's partner is screaming on the radio for help."

"I have a feeling I know how this ends." Magnus rubbed his hand over his face.

"Dispatch waited to pass on the information. Available units waited to respond. Adam bled to death in his partner's arms," Melissa finished.

"Fuck," Magnus spat.

"There was a massive cover-up. The partner ended up walking away from it all."

"I don't blame him," Magnus said.

"A couple of months after everything had been swept under the rug, I heard a captain in my division talking about the incident. They called it an 'incident'. They blamed Adam for not bailing on his partner when he had the chance," she told him. "This captain had a copy of the radio transmission. I found it in his desk."

"You went into your superior's desk?"

"They were laughing about the death of a fellow officer," she defended herself.

"I would have done the same thing," Magnus said.

"After I listened to it, I couldn't put up with it any longer. It changed me. The desperation in Tr...the partner's voice. I will never forget it," Melissa confessed.

"So, you started making waves," he said.

"Yes."

"So, that's why I hired you," Magnus told her. "And I expect you to do the same thing here."

She snapped her gaze to his.

"There is something going on in my town. Now, I'm not saying the park rangers are involved, but if they are, I'll take them down. You're going to help me."

"I will." Melissa nodded. "Yes."

"Good," Magnus said. "Let me introduce you to Deputy Wilson. He'll bring you up to speed."

"I'm excited to get started," she told him. It was the truth.

"One more thing." Magnus rose from the desk.

"Yes?"

"Were you sleeping with Adam or the partner?"

Damn, how does he know? Melissa turned to face her boss. "The partner."

"The shifter," Magnus clarified.

She nodded.

"And what happened with him?"

"Nothing I'm proud of," she said.

Magnus walked over then shocked her by patting her shoulder. "We all make mistakes. But at least I understand more now. I'm happy to have you as part of the team."

Chapter Two

Melissa's first week at the sheriff's office was eventful. Magnus did have a strong dislike for the two park rangers who had been in and out of the office. Melissa wasn't sure whether the rangers were involved in the recent hike in illegal hunting, but if not, then they weren't taking the threat seriously.

Magnus had stated he wasn't surprised, since they were human.

She didn't know if Magnus didn't trust all humans, or only the ones he dealt with. So far, he'd treated Melissa with respect, often asking her opinion on important matters. The other new deputy's arrival had been postponed for another couple of days, so she was still working mainly with Deputy Wilson.

This was the first time Melissa had been invited out with her co-workers. Logan's girlfriend worked at the bar on the edge of town. Melissa hadn't met her yet, but Logan brought her up often. Melissa hoped she'd find a friend in Annabelle. Not only did Melissa not know anyone in town other than the men she worked with, but it was turning out to be hard to connect with the residents of Brookside. Magnus had told her to give it time.

Apparently, the citizens of her new town found it hard to trust people.

Melissa understood—she did—but it was getting lonely.

In LA, when most of her fellow officers had started giving her the cold shoulder, she'd still had friends outside the police force. Being in a new place equaled starting over. Which was what she'd wanted, but Melissa would have preferred to be liked here.

She followed Carl Wilson inside the bar named The Den.

It was as she'd expected to find in a small California town out in the middle of nowhere. The place was pretty busy for a Friday night. The music wasn't too loud, though.

At a corner table sat Magnus, Logan and the two junior agents with the Coalition, Fredrick and Fabian. Melissa had liked the twins as soon as she'd met them. Fabian was loud, flirty and fun. He was also dating Carl. Fredrick, more serious than Fabian, was smart and nice. He'd even casually mentioned them getting dinner some time. Although Melissa wasn't ready to date and didn't want to mix her personal relationships with work, it was nice to be noticed.

The pretty woman behind the bar waved at them before pointing to the table with their co-workers.

Must be Annabelle.

She was supposed to be a feline shifter. Melissa tried to see if she could pick up any signs the young woman was a shifter.

She moved with grace, but that could have been from years of experience waiting tables. There was nothing screaming shifter to Melissa.

"Glad you could join us," Magnus said as she and Carl reached the table.

Fabian pulled Carl down next to him.

"Thank you for inviting me," Melissa replied. She sat in the empty chair between Magnus and Logan. That gave her the opportunity to see the entire bar, including the entrance.

"I brought beers." The woman from behind the bar walked to the table holding a tray of bottles. "Anyone want something different?"

Everyone around the table shook their heads, including Melissa.

"Good. I'm on a break now." She passed around the drinks. When she set one in front of Melissa, she smiled. "I'm Annabelle."

"Hi, I'm Melissa."

"I know," Annabelle said. "I've wanted to come meet you, but Logan wouldn't let me visit the station." Annabelle nudged her boyfriend.

Logan wrapped his arm around Annabelle's waist, then pulled her onto his lap. "Because I wouldn't get any work done with you around." He kissed her neck.

Annabelle laughed while smacking his hand. She turned to Melissa. "How're you settling in?"

"Good," Melissa replied. "It's a big change from Los Angeles, but for the better, I think."

"I could never live in a big city," Annabelle said. "I love my town too much."

"You'd never leave the bar unless it was to climb your tree, if you didn't have to," Logan said.

Annabelle shrugged at his teasing. "True."

"I was born and raised in LA," Melissa told her. "I didn't think towns like this actually existed."

"Well, I'm glad they do," Logan stated. "It's nice."

"You'd live in a cave if Annabelle wanted," Magnus remarked.

Logan flipped Magnus off. "You're one to talk. You don't leave Brookside, either."

Melissa enjoyed the teasing between co-workers. She'd had that once. Hopefully, she would again.

"There is no reason to leave here, ever," Magnus stated. "No one should."

She'd noticed the people she met seemed to have an unusual attachment to this town. Melissa wasn't certain if that was a shifter thing or not. Brookside wasn't picturesque. The buildings were rundown, the streets needed repairs and, with only two hundred residents, businesses weren't exactly booming. Still, there was something about the place that called to her. It seemed she wasn't the only one.

"You're staying in the old Windham place, right?" Annabelle asked.

"I am," Melissa said. "It is a beautiful house and it came furnished."

"Mary Windham moved to Colorado with her daughter after her husband died." Magnus picked up his bottle and drank. "She was a good woman."

"She took good care of the place. I've always lived in an apartment. I was kind of worried that I wouldn't be able to manage a place so big, but I like it. Last night, I drank a glass of wine, sitting on the back porch. It was so peaceful."

Annabelle picked up the bottle she'd brought Logan. She tipped it to Melissa. "It is peaceful here. Have you gone into the state park yet?"

"I found a running trail not far from my house," Melissa told her. "It takes me about two miles into the park."

"Oh! I know the trail," Annabelle said.

"I'm hoping to explore a little more. I printed out some maps of the area."

"If you need a guide, just let me know," Annabelle said. "I probably know every inch of the forest."

Leaning back in her chair, Melissa sipped at her beer. "That would be great." *See, I can make friends.* Annabelle seemed to be nice and Melissa had a good feeling about her.

It might not have been what she'd had in LA, but Melissa didn't think she'd ever be ready for relationships like that again. After Melissa had started to look into cases where shifters were being treated unfairly by the LAPD, her so-called friends had turned their backs on her.

The pain of betrayal remained with her even to this day.

"What are you doing Sunday?" Annabelle asked.

"Uh, no plans."

"So?"

Melissa cocked her head. "So?"

"Do you want to go hiking Sunday?"

"That might not be a good idea," Logan said. "We haven't had any trouble for about a week, but that doesn't mean it's safe."

Annabelle huffed. "We'll go hiking on only marked trails. In the morning. There won't be hunters out."

Logan shook his head. "One stray bullet..."

"I'm not going to stop visiting my trees because people suck," Annabelle argued.

For the first time since she'd begun working at the Brookside Sheriff Department, Melissa understood why Magnus seemed obsessed with keeping the state park safe. It was the people of Brookside who were suffering. Annabelle couldn't go for a run because she might get shot at. *Logan must live in constant fear for her safety.* It wasn't as simple as handing out tickets for illegal hunting. The threat was real. People, good people, could be killed.

"Be careful," Logan told Annabelle.

Annabelle grinned before turning to Melissa. "You in?"

"Yes!" Melissa said. Excitement built as she thought about navigating around her new home.

"Great. So, is there a man living in that big house with you?" Annabelle asked.

Melissa didn't miss the way the question drew the attention of the entire table. She looked around. "Uh, no man right now," she admitted.

"So, you left a poor broken-hearted guy back in LA?" Fabian questioned.

"Nothing like that," Melissa said. She avoided looking at Magnus. Ever since she'd let the only man she'd ever loved slip through her fingers, Melissa hadn't given any thought to her love life. It just didn't seem important — she needed to make amends for what she'd done first.

"Don't worry — we can gossip on Sunday," Annabelle said. "Without all these men listening in."

Melissa laughed. It felt good to have a friend again.

"There's Trent!" Annabelle said. "Trent!" She waved.

Melissa glanced up and almost dropped her beer bottle. *Oh, God! It can't be.* After years and years of searching, there was no way. But it was. He had the same swagger as he sauntered across the bar floor.

He looked up and their gazes locked. Trent froze.

She'd know those clear blue eyes anywhere.

"What's the matter with him?" Annabelle asked. She rose, but Trent wasn't looking at her. No, he hadn't taken his eyes off Melissa.

Melissa stood. "Trent."

In a flash, he'd turned on his heel and was storming through an open doorway, back further into the bar.

"What the—?" Annabelle said.

But Melissa didn't stop to think about her actions or what the others thought. She rushed after Trent, not even pausing to look over her shoulder as Magnus called her name.

Melissa skidded around the corner and almost crashed into a big biker guy.

"Hey, there," he said, grasping her upper arms to catch her from falling. "Slow down."

She jerked out of his hold. "Sorry, sorry." Melissa tried to go around him.

"I'm sorry, Miss, but customers can't be back here," he told her.

"Please." Melissa looked up at the big guy. "I have to get to him."

The man frowned. "Who?"

"Trent," she answered. "I need to catch him before he takes off."

"Trent." He looked behind him. It appeared he was trying to decide whether he'd let her through.

"You don't know me," she said. "I understand. But I need to talk to him."

"I don't think that's wise. Trent didn't look like he wanted company."

"He probably doesn't." Melissa blew the hair out of her face. "But I still need to talk to him."

The man peered at her as if he could see the secrets she was trying to hide. Melissa was so desperate to catch up to Trent she didn't care. "He went out of the back door. Just go through the kitchen. If he went into the forest, you won't find him," he said.

"I have to try," she responded.

"My name's Mac. Trent works for me. He's also a friend."

"Okay."

"I don't want to see him hurt."

Melissa met the biker's gaze. "I'm hoping to fix some of the hurt he's already been given."

With great reluctance, Mac stepped aside. "You better hurry."

She didn't waste time. Melissa high-tailed it down the hall and through the large kitchen. The woman cutting vegetables didn't even look up at her.

"Please," she whispered. Melissa banged open the back door and ran through. She skidded to a stop when she saw him.

Trent was pacing back and forth on the other side of a picnic table that separated them.

"No." He shook his head. "No."

"Trent." She held up her hands. "I want to talk to you."

"Why are you here?" he yelled. The pain lacing his voice hurt Melissa. "This is my place. My family! You're not supposed to be here."

"I'm sorry." God, she was sorry. Melissa had gone over what she'd say to Trent if she ever saw him again, but all the words had left having to face him in reality. He seemed so much the same, but different.

Instead of the brilliant smile he'd always given her, his jaw was set and his lips pressed together. His light-brown hair was longer than she'd ever seen it. *And his body...* Dear God, he'd bulked up. In a pair of faded jeans and a tight black T-shirt, he looked fantastic.

"What are you doing here?" he demanded.

"I didn't know you were here." She stepped forward, but he shuffled back several feet. "I swear I didn't know you were here."

"And you just happened to show up where I live?" he asked. "I don't fucking believe you."

Melissa had picked up enough talk at the office to know The Den was not only a bar but housed several shifters from the area. The way Magnus and Logan often stopped talking when she walked into a room had made her suspicious that more was going on than she was aware of. Anytime The Den was mentioned, Magnus and Logan exchanged looks.

"Answer me!" he shouted.

"I didn't know you were here," Melissa said. "I joined the Brookside Sheriff Department a week ago. I was only having a beer with my co-workers when you walked in."

"You're the new deputy?" Trent went pale.

"I didn't know!" Melissa would beg for him to believe her.

"You work for a town full of shifters," Trent said. "Is this a fucking joke?"

"No." Melissa tried again to get closer. Trent seemed so lost in thought he didn't react this time. "I've changed."

"You changed," Trent barked.

"I—"

He pointed a finger at her. "Stay the fuck away from me." Then he turned and stomped off into the forest.

Melissa thought about following him but knew that if Trent wasn't ready to talk, there wasn't anything she could do about it. But now she knew where he was. Melissa dropped down on the bench of the picnic table.

Trent. Here.

How in the hell had she gotten so lucky?

When he'd first taken off out of LA, Melissa had been relieved. God help her, but she had been glad the stress and drama from Adam's murder would end. Since she'd first started dating Trent, she'd become fast friends with Adam. Her and Trent and Adam and his wife often double-dated.

She'd lost Adam the night he'd been killed, but she'd lost Trent as well.

Trent had gone nuts when the Medical Examiner had pronounced Adam dead on scene. It had taken eight officers to get Trent down and under control.

Later that night, when Trent had gone to her apartment looking for comfort, was when she'd made the biggest mistake of her life. The things she'd said to Trent still made her sick. It didn't matter she'd been afraid, having received threats earlier that day. She'd turned her back on him when Trent had needed her the most.

What Melissa had done still haunted her.

She rose and, instead of going back into the bar, headed around the building. She couldn't face anyone at the moment. These were Trent's friends. No, he had called them his family. While she'd been trying to take on the entire LAPD, he'd been only hours away, hiding in Brookside.

Melissa couldn't get over the pain she'd seen in Trent's eyes the moment he'd spotted her.

Just seeing her again had hurt him.

She'd screwed up.

Her hand shook as she pulled her car keys from her pocket. All she could do was think of her next step. Melissa didn't know if she should even remain in Brookside. Trent didn't want her there.

But if she could explain?

Prove to Trent she wasn't the same person who'd betrayed his love?

They might never get back together. Hell, for all she knew, Trent could be married by now. But, in order to sleep at night, she needed to at least say she was sorry, and when he was listening. Not being freaked out after seeing her again.

Melissa yanked open her car door.

She had no clue where to go from here.

* * * *

Trent walked for an hour before making his way back toward the bar. He spotted the tree Annabelle had climbed the night three hunters had been shooting at her. He dropped down on a fallen log and hung his head. That was as good a place as any to try to figure out what the hell was going on.

Melissa Bishop. In my town.

He felt as though he'd fallen down a rabbit hole. *And damn, Melissa looks good.* Just like he remembered, all the nights she came to him in his dreams.

"Oh, God." He managed to choke back the sob trying to force its way out. He wouldn't give her or anyone from his old life the satisfaction of ever breaking down again.

"I thought I might find you here."

Trent jolted. He hadn't heard Annabelle approach. No one ever snuck up on him. But with his mind on Melissa, he hadn't been keeping track of his surroundings. That was dangerous. "What are you doing out here?" He was glad his voice was even.

"Checking on you," she replied. "You have a lot of people worried."

"I'm fine," he snapped. Trent didn't want anyone to worry about him. He wasn't a victim. Trent wouldn't ever be a victim again.

Instead of leaving like he hoped, she came around and peered down. He wanted to growl and demand she leave him alone, but he couldn't. Not to Annabelle. She was like his little sister.

"Trent," she said softly.

"I can't," he whispered. He couldn't talk about Melissa right then. Not with her surprising arrival so fresh.

"You don't have to." Annabelle came forward before dropping down between his legs. She laid her head on his leg. "I just want to sit with you."

Trent ran his fingers through Annabelle's silky hair. She was the first person who'd ever seen him as anything more than some unhinged shifter. She also had never been afraid of him. Even though she was the size of a house cat in her shifted form, she still didn't react negatively to his hyena.

Annabelle also didn't know anything about his past. She knew he was an ex-cop, but not from here. Trent didn't like to talk about Adam or what had happened with the LAPD and she hadn't pressed. That meant the world to him.

"I didn't think I'd ever see her again," Trent murmured.

Annabelle didn't reply.

"But fuck, she looked good, didn't see?"

Still nothing.

Trent smiled. "I bet you're dying to know what's going on."

She turned her cheek on his knee and looked up at him. "Don't leave us."

"What?" Trent frowned.

"If you run, I'll never see you again."

"You think I'll take off on you?" he asked. Not that she was wrong. He'd been thinking that while he'd walked. He could be out of this town in an hour.

After he'd left LA, he'd traveled around quite a lot. The first year, he'd been unsettled and angry. It hadn't mattered where he'd gone or how much trouble he found. Trent couldn't let go of the injustice of Adam's killing and cover-up.

He'd been headed back to LA to take out every single officer who'd refused to come to Adam's aid that night. A stop for a drink at The Den had changed his life. Mac had seen the pain Trent had been in. When Mac wanted to make someone part of his family, it was almost impossible to resist.

A bed for the night had turned into another, then another.

When Trent had been ready to walk out of the door, a case had come in. Trent hadn't had any idea about the underground network Mac ran from the bar. But seeing the young teenage boy shaking in fear from the humans who had been threatening him had stopped Trent in his tracks.

He'd had a decision to make. Go forward with his plan on revenge or help someone who needed him. Trent had chosen to stay with Mac. He'd been there ever since.

Now he was considering leaving his home because of a woman.

A woman he'd once thought he'd spend the rest of his life with once.

Annabelle had her eyes closed, but he knew she wasn't asleep. If he even so much as twitched, she'd respond. "Did you love her?" she asked.

"Yes." He didn't have it in him to deny what Melissa had meant to him.

"But she hurt you?"

"Yes," he said again.

"Then I hate her."

Trent chuckled. "I don't want you to hate her."

"Too late."

"She's not a bad person," Trent said. "And it was a long time ago."

"Doesn't matter. I hate her and will never talk to her again."

Trent pulled on a strand of her hair. She was a brat and he loved her for it.

"No one gets to hurt you," Annabelle declared. She opened her eyes. "I saw your face when you spotted her."

"I wasn't expecting it," Trent confessed. "I never thought I'd see her again."

"But she works here now. With Magnus. Logan says she's dedicated to helping with the hunting issues," Annabelle said.

Trent snorted. *Melissa helping shifters? Melissa despises shifters.*

"Do you think she followed you here?" Annabelle asked. "I'll have Magnus arrest her. Or Logan. He'll put her in federal custody."

He had to smile. Annabelle would be a pain in the ass to Magnus or Logan if they didn't do what she wanted. "They have no reason to arrest her."

"They could make one up."

"She works for Magnus. I don't think he'd lock up his own deputy because you told him to."

"Then he'll fire her, make her go away."

No one defended him like Annabelle. He wished she'd been in LA. Or no, he didn't. Annabelle belonged in Brookside, safe and protected. "I don't want her fired." Or at least not until he did some recon for himself. "And I don't want you to hate her, so be nice."

She blew out a breath. "Fine."

"I bet you know where she lives, though," he said.

Annabelle beamed. "Can I go with you?"

"No."

"Oh, come on!" Annabelle whined. "I want to see, too."

"Not this time," he told her.

Annabelle huffed. "She's renting the Windham place."

Well, shit. Melissa was less than a fifteen-minute walk from him. "Okay." He motioned for her to move.

"You promise you're coming back?" she asked.

"Yes." Trent helped her to her feet. "I promise."

"If you don't, I'll have Magnus or Logan arrest you," she threatened.

"Okay." He kissed her forehead. "I'll be back later. Tell everyone else I'm fine."

"And to leave you alone?" she asked.

Trent nudged her toward the bar. "You better get back before Logan starts to worry."

She dragged her feet but started forward. "One more question."

"Just one," he said.

"Why did you come here?" She pointed toward the tree.

"To remind me why I'm still here in town."

"Okay." Annabelle walked away and Logan watched until she was out of sight. Yeah, she was the sister he'd never had. It would be hard to leave her. But if Melissa was there to stay, how could he?

Trent pulled off his clothes and wedged them under the log. He set his boots on top to hold them down. Then he crouched, so he could call forth his hyena form.

The transformation was instant.

One minute, he had toes and fingers, and the next, his body was covered in fur.

As a spotted hyena, Trent had often been mistaken for a dog in the past. But around these parts, with other shifters, most knew what he was. He had never gotten respect growing up because of what he could shift into. Here in Brookside, for the first time, he could transform without the worry of being attacked.

He didn't shift often, still not comfortable after years of being bullied, but every once in a while, he let his hyena free.

Trent knew where the house Melissa was staying was located.

He trotted along, not following the path. He knew a shortcut that would take him to the back fence of the Windham house. It felt good to stretch his legs and put on some speed. He didn't get the same thrill as

Annabelle did from running in this forest, but he still enjoyed it. Trent's favorite part of letting his hyena free was the solace he found in the quiet trees surrounding him, as though the branches and trees protected him.

Trent slowed as he reached the first house in the neighborhood. Melissa's place was four houses down the street, or alley, like he was strolling down. It was still early enough in the night that there was a chance he'd run into someone. Mitzi Phelps lived next to Melissa. Mitzi had been one of Trent's one-night stands. On the other side of the street was the Johnson family. Their oldest had been visiting last Christmas and Trent had spent an evening keeping her warm.

The interactions he'd had with the women in the area might be an issue, at least for Melissa. Trent didn't have any regrets. She'd been the one who'd left him, after all.

Trent liked this part of town.

The houses were two stories and well taken care of, the yards big with plenty of room for kids or shifters to play in. There was also a good deal of space between the residences, so even with shifter hearing, there should be privacy allocated to the home owners.

Trent slowed, passing Mitzi's house until he was right at the edge of Melissa's property. He stopped before lying on his stomach. Melissa sat on the back steps with a glass of wine. She wiped her face with the back of her hand. She was crying.

An ache grew in his chest.

Even after how they'd ended things, he didn't want her upset. He thought he'd at least have fallen out of love with her, Melissa's betrayal had cut so deep. But watching her, Trent had to wonder if his feelings would ever go away.

She was still so beautiful. Melissa used to wear her dark-brown hair pulled back most of the time. It was only at night, when they were wrapped in each other's arms that he could play with her long strands. Now, she sported a cute short bob.

Melissa's hair had been down the night everything had fallen apart, when he'd gone to her apartment with Adam's blood still coating his clothes. He could still see her fresh from the shower wearing a robe and her hair still wet.

"What are you doing here, Trent?" Melissa had asked.

"I needed to make sure you're okay." Trent had tried to take her in his arms, but Melissa had side-stepped out of the way.

"You shouldn't be here," Melissa had stated.

"Adam…"

"I know about Adam," she'd said. Tears had gathered in her eyes. "Everyone knows about Adam."

"They let him die," Trent had yelled.

"Did they?" she'd shouted. "Or did you?"

He'd felt like he'd been slapped. "What?"

"You knew how everyone felt," she'd screamed. "And you still let him be your partner. You did this!"

"No!" he'd howled. She couldn't think that about him. Melissa wasn't like all the others. "I loved Adam like a brother."

"Well, now your brother's dead!"

He'd staggered. He couldn't have been more surprised if he'd been shot. A year and a half. They'd been together for a year and a half. In all that time, it had only been in the last three months that anyone had known he was a shifter. Trent had been one of the first to come out to the LAPD as being a shifter. He'd figured with the public support, the men and women he'd worked with would accept him.

And his naivety had cost his best friend his life.

Now, not only was Adam gone, but Melissa had looked at him with hate in her eyes. Trent barely managed to keep a howl of rage from escaping. He shook his head to clear away the memory. He'd left Melissa's apartment and she hadn't tried to stop him. Out of everything he'd lost that night, Melissa's face as she'd screamed Adam's death was his fault had stuck with him.

He backed away. He needed to return to his family. There was a lot of thinking he had to do. This time Trent raced from Melissa, but he wasn't letting the despair and anger lead him. No, he had people who cared about him. They might be shifters, monsters to the LAPD, but they were his family. He fit with them.

Trent made it back to the log in record time. He skidded to a stop in front of Mac, who held his clothes.

"That didn't take long," Mac said.

Trent shook his entire body.

"Annabelle told me where you were going. She also said you wanted to be left alone."

Trent began his transformation. It wasn't like he could respond to Mac as an animal. "This is you giving me space?"

"No, this is me checking to make sure you come back."

"I promised Annabelle I would," Trent snapped.

"And I know you wouldn't break your word to her," Mac said. "It doesn't mean I don't worry, about both of you. Annabelle needs to be able to trust your word. If you hadn't been able to keep that promise, I needed to know so I could protect her and make her understand you weren't abandoning her."

"Doesn't it get tiresome always watching over us?" Trent asked. He'd often wondered but had never dared question Mac. He needed Mac to push him and be his friend.

"No, it's what I need to do."

Well, that makes sense. Mac's need to control the environment his family was in stemmed from the death of his sister.

"Do you want to talk about it?" Mac offered.

"And say what? The woman I wanted to marry and who blames me for my best friend's death just showed up in town and I'm okay with it? Because I'm not."

"I wouldn't expect you to be."

Trent grabbed his clothes from Mac and pulled them on. He sat on the log to get his boots on but stopped and sighed. "I thought I was done with that part of my life."

"I know you did," Mac said.

"It's not fair."

"No, but life is rarely fair. We both know that," Mac replied. "Magnus had no idea. He knew she was from LAPD, but not that you were."

"I know," Trent said. "It's not his fault."

"So, what are you going to do?"

Trent peered around the forest. Could he find another home like this one? He doubted it. He sighed. "I have no idea. No fucking clue."

Chapter Three

Melissa paused with her hand on the doorknob of the sheriff's office. As much as she'd wanted to call in sick, Melissa wasn't a coward. Everyone had to know her past with Trent by now. Melissa would look them in the eye, even if Sheriff Magnus fired her. At least she'd have the weekend to figure out what to do next.

She pushed open the door and—no surprise—everyone turned to her.

"Hey, Melissa." Fabian was the first to greet her.

"Hey." She looked around. Magnus and Logan were in their offices but had glanced up at her entrance. Fabian, Fredrick and Carl were sitting around the desk, hanging out, it appeared. Magnus motioned her to him.

Melissa didn't bother to drop off her bag. She went directly to her boss' office. "You wanted to see me?" she asked from the doorway.

"I did. Close the door."

Magnus never wanted his door closed. "Yes, sir." She followed his order, then stood and braced herself.

"Sit down."

Well, shit. If Magnus was going to fire her, she'd rather be on her feet. She opened her mouth.

"Relax, Deputy," Magnus said. "I merely want to talk to you."

"Sure." She sat in the terrible chair and peered at him.

"I owe you an apology," he said.

"A what?" Melissa had no idea what was going on. An apology for firing her? Well, at least Magnus had a heart. She had no idea where she'd go from here. Sure, she was only renting her house, but Melissa didn't have anywhere else to go. All the bridges she'd burned to get here didn't leave many choices.

"I didn't know who Trent was. I don't run the people Mac takes under his protection unless they cause problems in town. It's a deal we have. Mac does good work and the men and women who come to him are usually running from something. As long as they keep their noses clean, I leave them alone."

"You had no way of knowing," she said. "None of us could have."

"Still, I've managed to put you in a pretty uncomfortable situation."

She nodded.

"And I don't mean to sound callous, but I need to know if you're going to stay."

"Stay?"

Magnus sighed. "I understand if you don't want to remain in your position. I'd hate to see you leave. We were finally making some leeway on the illegal hunting. You're a smart investigator and with the other deputy still not here, you leaving would set us back."

"You're not firing me?"

"Fire you? What for? Having an ex-boyfriend?"

Melissa shook her head. "Because Trent was here first? I'm sure the people at the bar realized I had a past with him."

"It was discussed, although the details were not shared. I don't think anyone but Mac is aware of what happened."

"So, Trent's boss knows?"

"Yes, we discussed it."

"And he didn't demand I be let go?" She could still hear the deep voice telling her he didn't want Trent hurt again.

"He doesn't tell me how to run my department," Magnus stated.

"I really thought you were going to fire me."

"I have no reason to can your ass."

"Everyone is going to hate me," Melissa said. "Or they do already."

"It won't be easy," Magnus responded. "Trent is part of Mac's pack. Everyone around here loves Mac."

"Great," she muttered.

"You've come from a place that tried to burn you at the stake like you're a witch. If you can get through that, then this shouldn't be a problem."

"Except, when I was in LA, I knew I was on the right side of things. Here...I'm totally in the wrong," she admitted.

"You've put in years trying to make up for your mistakes. I respect that."

"I don't think anyone else will see it that way."

"Maybe not. But you never know. I've seen the citizens of Brookside band together time and time again to do what's right. You probably won't have anyone being openly friendly to you, but they won't be hateful either."

"That'll keep me warm at night," she said.

Magnus chuckled. "I have plenty of paperwork you can take home with you for company. Just don't throw it into the fireplace."

She sighed with relief. Sitting back in her chair, she wanted to thank Magnus but knew the sheriff wouldn't like it. "I promise," she said instead.

"Now, we haven't had a situation with illegal hunting since you've been here, which is good, but makes me think that it's merely a matter of time. The other deputy will be starting on Monday, but this weekend, we need to keep a close eye on things," Magnus said. "I'm making a rotation for all of us to be out in the forest. Even the Coalition."

"I'll do my part," she promised.

"I never doubted you. Now, go get to work,' Magnus ordered.

Melissa stood and, with her bag in hand, walked toward the door. She paused. Hell, she had to say it. "Thank you." She didn't look at him as she spoke.

"You're welcome."

Once back at her desk, she glanced around. Carl was going over maps with Fabian, but Fredrick was very deliberately not looking at her. It could be nothing, but she had a feeling it was going to be awkward in the office. *Doesn't matter, I have a job to do.*

She logged on to her computer to get started for the day. Opening her email, she saw Magnus had sent the rotation for everyone in the office to patrol the state park that night. She was on from midnight to two in the morning, with Carl on shift before her and Fredrick after. Even Logan was slotted for a spot.

Attached to the email was a map of highlighted sections to concentrate on.

"Fab, get in here!" Logan yelled.

Melissa glanced over her shoulder. Logan might have been talking to Fabian, but he was frowning at her.

"What's up, boss?" Fabian asked as he sauntered toward Logan.

"I told you not to call me boss." Logan pushed Fabian into his office, then slammed the door.

"What'd he do this time?" Carl asked.

"I don't know," Fredrick replied. "Logan's been in a bad mood all morning." He side-eyed Melissa.

Logan's attitude must be her fault, too. She sighed. It was going to be a long-ass day. But she had things she could look into to keep her mind off the only thing, or person, she wanted to think about.

There was no telling what Trent was doing. Or even how he spent his time around this small town.

Mac's people, that was what Magnus had called Trent.

There was something there.

She'd thought before that Mac had some kind of connection to the people of the Brookside no one talked about.

Well, no one's going to talk to me now.

Making friends was going to be a whole lot harder than before. But at least she had her job and she'd do it to the best of her ability. She'd learned a lot in the past few years, having to work mostly alone. Even if the other deputies and Coalition agents didn't want her around, she had a boss who was supporting her. It was more than she'd had in LA. Magnus wanted the citizens of their town safe, and that would be her mission. She was good at channeling all her energy into work.

If the residents of Brookside wanted to shift and go for a run in the protected state park, they had the right.

Melissa would see to it they remained safe. Maybe, over time, she would stop being disgusted with herself.

* * * *

Trent's feet pounded on the concrete as the sound echoed around him. He hadn't been able to sleep. Again. So instead of shifting and running through the forest, he was trying to wear himself out the old-fashioned way.

He'd taken a long ride on his Harley with Duffy and Calvin as company. The three of them worked well as a unit. As a member of Mac's underground group, it was their job to handle the dangerous parts. Annabelle could calm even the most frightened person. Carter ferreted out intel that even the Pentagon would have trouble locating. Kelly kept all of them fed and Mac ran the entire outfit like a military op.

There were other residents in town who helped from time to time, but for the most part, the inner circle took care of day-to-day work.

Without anyone in need of their services, Mac had let them go on a ride. Duffy and Calvin were perfect companions. They liked talking almost as much as he did, which was as little as possible. So he'd been able to enjoy the scenery up to the coast. It hadn't helped, though. Seeing Melissa again was fucking with his mind.

So, here he was at two in the morning, after closing the bar, trying to get his thoughts back to where it'd been before Melissa had come into his life again. Leaving town was on the back burner at the moment. Annabelle hadn't left his side all night. And really, Trent didn't want to go. But a break might be in order.

He could travel to some of the safe houses they had set up and check on the residents. Trent would have to run his idea by Mac, after his boss woke up.

"Unbelievable," Trent muttered. "This is my home and I'm not leaving." He'd started to talk to himself again. He'd done it in the early days after leaving LA, and now here he was again. He turned to head back toward the bar and his bed. He'd worked up quite a sweat. A shower then hopefully a few hours of shut-eye.

Trent had to resist the urge to veer off into the street that would take him in front of Melissa's house. It would be too easy. Melissa didn't even have to know. But Trent would. If he didn't avoid all contact with Melissa, there was a good chance Trent would do something he'd regret later.

Like seeing if Melissa still tasted as good as she used to.

He picked up his pace for the last mile back to the bar. Just as he was rounding the corner to the back door, he heard a loud shot.

"Fuck!" Trent raced toward the forest. If the hunters were out and shooting at someone or something, he was going to tear their heads off.

He heard a crash behind him as the back door of the bar was thrown open, but Trent didn't stop to see who was joining him.

Another shot. Someone was using a shotgun.

There was a shout, but he was too far away to understand what had been said. Trent growled. He was really trying to not blame all humans for the world's stupidity, but it was getting hard. Even Melissa had put her humanity before what was right. She'd had no trouble turning her back on him.

He burst through the branches, pushing them away from his face. A few cracked or swatted back at him, but it didn't matter. He had to get to the hunters before they disappeared again.

A third shot.

Oh, hell, no! A natural animal or shifter could be in real danger. This was also close to where Annabelle had been attacked before. Hopefully Logan had her inside and in bed.

Trent took off at full speed. The closer he got, the more commotion he heard.

"Sheriff's department! Drop your weapon." The shout was loud and clear this time.

Oh, God no, Melissa's there, too. Probably dealing with the same hunters Magnus thought were targeting shifters. Trent desperately hurried forward. He was wearing down, though.

A fourth shot.

Shit! Trent used every last ounce of energy to propel himself deeper into the forest. He leapt over fallen limbs and came out between a smaller cluster of trees.

Melissa stood in a ready-to-fire stance over a man on the ground. The scent of blood was strong.

Melissa jolted as he crashed through, bringing her gun up in defense, aimed at him.

"It's only me," Trent panted. He bent over with his hands on his knees. "I heard the shots."

"Damn." Melissa let out a deep breath while lowering her weapon.

A rifle had fallen a couple of yards from where the guy was passed out cold on the ground.

"What's going on?" Trent asked.

Melissa huffed. Her hands shook as she repositioned herself to cover the hunter. "I was patrolling and heard a shot then...a...roar? I followed the sound and came across the man trying to shoot a cat of some kind. Not a tiger or lion. The animal knocked this guy down and clawed at him before taking off."

"Was it a natural animal or shifter?" Trent questioned.

"I have no idea. All I know is it came from some kind of feline," Melissa said. She'd gone a little pale. He hoped she didn't pass out. "I don't think the animal was hurt, though. I tried to call out to it, but it ran off."

Trent strolled closer. He could pick up the scent of the feline. He recognized it, but didn't say anything to Melissa. She didn't know the residents, and they wouldn't talk to her. He needed to see Magnus. "Was he alone?" Trent waved a hand at the human.

"I don't think so," she answered. "There was more than one weapon fired. I could tell when I was running over here. The other person was gone by the time I arrived, though."

"Okay," Trent said. "I need to look around."

"Uh." Melissa motioned toward the human. "I'll secure this guy and call in to the sheriff." Melissa rushed to the human and checked his pulse. "I think he's only knocked out. The blood is from a gash in his arm."

"He'll be fine." Trent should care about the human, but his issues were growing. He never thought he'd be the kind of shifter who started to hate all humans. That was not who he wanted to become.

"Magnus," she said. "Come in, Sheriff." Melissa was calling Magnus by radio. She was human. Why didn't he hate her? Even after she'd broken him, Trent didn't hate her. He'd been trying to convince himself he did, though. Which was why he was standing in the forest and not in his own bed.

"What's going on, Deputy?" Magnus barked.

"We had an attack," she told him.

"Where? How bad?"

"Section one-ten," she replied. "I have one hunter down. I witnessed him shooting. He also took a shot at me."

Trent clenched his fist. The asshole had attacked Melissa as well? Now, he wanted to rip the guy apart. Melissa was human, just doing her job.

"Are you injured?" Magnus asked.

"No," Melissa reported. "The only injury is on our suspect."

"What kind of injury?" Magnus demanded.

"He's unconscious and claw-slash on his arm. I have him in cuffs."

"Claw-slash?" Magnus asked. "Is the animal okay?"

"Everything seems okay," she said. "The animal ran off. I don't think it was injured. Trent is here. He heard the shots."

"I'll be there in seven minutes," Magnus stated. "Keep the scene secure. Have Trent make sure there is nothing else going on around there."

"Yes, sir."

Trent wanted to smile. Melissa was peering around as if she expected the animal to jump out at any moment.

"Was it a shifter?" she asked.

"Yes," Trent admitted.

"What kind?"

"Cougar," Trent supplied.

"Oh!" Melissa gasped. She even took a few steps forward. "A cougar shifter. A resident?"

"Samuel Adams," Trent said. He might as well tell her. Magnus would need to know.

"Do you think he was hurt? Maybe I should send a deputy to check on him," Melissa said.

Trent was surprised by her words. This was the same woman who had blamed him for Adam's death because he hadn't quit the force after coming out as a shifter. He glanced away from Melissa. She wanted to make sure a shifter was uninjured. "I think it would be a good idea. I didn't pick up the smell of Sam's blood, but he might be shaken up. He lives on his own."

"Okay." Melissa picked up her radio.

"*Trent!*"

"Over here, Mac!" Trent yelled back.

Mac stomped into view only half-dressed.

"What took you so long?" Trent asked. It had to have been Mac who'd been going out of the back door of the bar. He should have arrived right after Trent.

"I thought I smelled someone else in the area. I followed the trail since I knew you were headed this way to help," Mac said. He narrowed his eyes at either the hunter or Melissa.

"Did you find anyone?" Trent asked.

"No," Mac said. "I followed the scent to the road where a car must have been waiting. It looks to me this guy hadn't been alone, but instead got left behind."

"So there were more of them?" Melissa asked. "I thought so."

"Yes. I can easily pick up another scent," Mac replied.

"That would have been helpful in the past." Melissa smiled. "Amazing."

Trent shook his head. *Who has Melissa turned into?*

"What's the guy's story?" Mac pointed to the stranger.

"Gerald Bono," Melissa said. "Twenty-two, lives in Alexandra, his hunting license is new. Only issued within the last month."

"Strange," Trent commented.

"This whole thing is strange," she replied. "It's like this area is being purposely targeted. The national park is protected. There are other places, closer to his home, he could have gone to hunt legally. Instead he traveled two hours to come here."

"Rifle's new, too," Mac said.

"What is going on?" Melissa leaned over the human. "Who are these guys?"

"Good question," Magnus said as he joined them. "One we're going to figure out."

Melissa straightened, the look on her face one of total professionalism. It was the same look she'd carried in LAPD. It made a chill crawl up his spine.

"Mac said he picked up the scent of another person in the area," she told her boss.

"Where?" Magnus demanded.

"There." Melissa pointed.

"Come on, Mac, show me. I'll be right back," Magnus said.

Trent found himself alone with Melissa. *Shit, I should have left as soon as Mac arrived.*

"Uh." Melissa peered around, not looking at him. "Carl is going to check on Sam. He already knew where he lived."

"Yeah," Trent agreed. "Small town." He walked around, trying to pick up more scents or clues. There was a bigger picture they were missing.

"Maybe you shouldn't be doing that."

"Why not?" Trent asked.

"There could be evidence," she said.

"You think I'm involved?"

"Of course not," Melissa cried. "Never."

"Then tell me what's going on," Trent demanded.

"I can't. It's part of an ongoing investigation and you're not a—"

"Not a what?" He stalked forward. "A cop? You're right. I'm not. But then I don't see you wearing the blue of the LAPD anymore."

"I made a mistake…"

Trent barked out a laugh.

"Trent." She moved forward. They were only inches apart. "The night you came to my apartment—"

"Don't," he spat. "Don't you fucking dare talk to me about that night."

She grabbed the front of his shirt. "I fucked up. I have no excuse. I'm sorry."

He wished her words meant something to him. Instead, all he could think about was the look on her face when she'd said Adam's death was his fault. "It doesn't matter." But it did.

"I didn't know," she said. "I didn't understand."

"And now you do?" he asked. He grew angry. Working with shifters for a week didn't give her the right to think she knew them.

"No," she said. Melissa lowered her voice. "I can't ever know what you feel or everything you went through. I do know what I did was wrong."

All this talk. Trent just wanted to go back to his room. He tried to step away, but she tightened her grip.

"After you left, I…"

"It doesn't matter," he said.

"It does. Please listen to me," she pleaded.

"Fine." He straightened his shoulders then pulled away from her. "Say what you want."

"I'm sorry," she said. "I was horrible and wrong. Adam's death wasn't your fault. Nothing was. It was everyone else. If I'd been stronger, I would have been at your side like I should have been. Instead I turned my back on you. I'm so sorry."

"You keep saying that," he commented.

"Because you're not listening," she responded. "But I'll say it again and again until you believe me."

Trent snorted. "You think you'll have the chance?"

"I hope I do."

He shook his head.

"I've tried to make amends for what I did," she told him.

"You thinking working for a town full of shifters will fix everything?" he asked. Was that what Melissa hoped to accomplish? Get rid of her guilt by working there? That was too little too late for Trent.

"Maybe not," Melissa said. "Hopefully I can make a difference here, though."

"Fine." Trent glanced around. He could see Mac, Logan and Annabelle standing out of sight from Melissa. Magnus would be returning soon. "You do whatever it is that brought you here. Just stay away from me."

She pressed her lips together. "Is that what you really want?"

He hesitated.

"Or we could talk more? There is a lot to catch up on."

Is she fucking kidding? "If I get the urge to rip open any old wounds, I'll give you a call."

Melissa dropped her shoulders and looked at the ground. "Okay."

Trent stomped off. He passed Magnus but didn't even acknowledge the other man. It was late and he was fucking tired.

"Hey!"

Trent turned. Mac was hurrying up to him.

"What's up?" Trent asked.

"Heading back?"

"Yeah, I need a shower and my bed," Trent told him.

"I'll walk with you," Mac said.

"Really?" Trent frowned. "You think I need a babysitter."

"We're going to the same place. We can walk together," Mac told him.

"And I suppose you'll talk and I'll listen?" Trent asked.

"That's the plan." Mac grinned.

"Come on."

Mac walked forward so Trent fell in step with him. They'd only taken a dozen steps before Mac was glancing at him from the corner of his eye.

"You got until we get to the back door," Trent told him.

"Anything you want to talk about?" Mac threw back.

"No."

"Okay, then." Mac didn't seem surprised. "How about we talk about Melissa Bishop?"

"No."

"Magnus had a lot of applications he went through before even interviewing Melissa," Mac said.

Trent merely grunted.

"The potentials he was the most interested in he gave to me and I ran them through the databases we have access to. I'm sorry that I didn't connect her to you or Adam," Mac said.

"Why would you? As far as the LAPD was concerned, we were only co-workers." Damn it, Mac had reeled him into the conversation.

"But we both know you were more," Mac stated. It wasn't a question. "Even if you never told me her name, I would have known it was her the moment you saw her again. You sparked to life."

"Doesn't matter," Trent replied.

"I think it does." Mac stopped walking. "I asked Magnus if he was going to let her go."

"He doesn't have any grounds to fire her," Trent said.

"Maybe not, but I'm sure we could have come up with something. He told me no, anyway."

Was that relief Trent felt? He didn't know. As painful as it was to have Melissa close, he didn't want her gone either. *Shit, I'm all kinds of fucked up.* "Why bring it up?"

"I wanted to know your reaction. Now, I do."

"Damn it," Trent muttered.

"You can try to ignore Melissa, but this is a small town. Plus, there's a connection between the sheriff's department and our group. You're going to bump into her," Mac told her.

"I know."

"Which means no matter how much you don't want to deal with her, it's going to happen," Mac continued.

"I said I know."

"Magnus will fill us in on the investigation into the illegal hunting," Mac said. "If you want in, it'll be at the bar at noon."

"No problem," Trent said. "I'll be here." He started walking again.

"He's coming alone. Just us and him."

"That wasn't even a little bit subtle," Trent admonished.

"In case you were worried."

"I wasn't." The bar door of the bar came into view. It was still standing open, but Duffy, Carter and Calvin were on guard around the building. Trent waved at them, letting them know everything was okay.

"Did you kill anyone?" Duffy asked.

"Night's still young," Trent warned.

"Oh, yeah? You think you can take me?" Duffy danced around. "Come on, doggie."

Trent lunged, but Mac caught him around by the shoulder. He was pleased to see Duffy had flinched.

"Stop messing with him," Calvin told Duffy, pulling his boyfriend to his side.

"Come on! I want to hear him bark."

"I hate all of you," Trent muttered. He didn't. Duffy teasing him made Trent know he was part of the family. They all acted like immature teenagers when stressed out.

"No!" Duffy cried dramatically. "You're our brother now!"

"I am not!" Trent sounded outraged.

"You are!" Duffy exclaimed.

"I was crazy before I got here," Trent said. "What's your excuse?"

Duffy blew him a kiss.

"Go take your shower," Mac ordered. He pushed Trent toward inside.

"Fine." Trent waved his hand then walked to the door. He'd let the others in the group handle anything else Mac needed, although they should all be in bed by now. It was after three in the morning.

The inside of the bar was quiet. He didn't see Kelly anywhere, so she must have still been asleep. Good, there wasn't anything Kelly could have done.

He strolled down the hall until he reached his room. Trent stopped and laid his hand on the wood. He was tired of always going to bed all alone. Even when he had a visitor for the night, she didn't stay long. He hadn't spent an entire night with his arms wrapped around a woman since Melissa.

Trent turned then leaned against his door. He slid to the ground.

"Fuck." He couldn't make himself go inside. It didn't matter that the others would be walking by soon or that he really needed a shower.

Everything was jumbled in his brain. He hated Melissa, how she'd made him feel, for turning her back on him. But he'd loved her once. And maybe he still did. At least a little. He wanted to be disgusted and hate her. Instead, all he could think about was her going back to her big house all alone.

Someone had taken a shot at her. Had been hunting in his back yard. With the residents around town not trusting her, the only back-up Melissa had was her fellow deputies and sheriff.

Damn it. Trent banged his head on his door.

What were the chances of her showing up there, anyway? In a million years, he'd never have thought they'd be in the same place at the same time again. Brookside had saved him. Could it save her, too? Was that what Melissa was looking for?

So many questions. *So fucking many questions.*

He climbed to his feet. Trent couldn't let Melissa go back home alone. He'd shift and make sure she at least got inside her house safe.

Chapter Four

Melissa finished loading the dishwasher then closed the door and turned the machine on. She'd been relieved that the house had modern appliances. Even better, the place was like the home she'd had as a child. She was comfortable there.

She'd had a quick lunch of an egg salad sandwich and chips. It would have been a good idea to go to the grocery store, but she wasn't up for it. The residents were still going to look at her funny. When she'd been walking patrol, they'd ignored her. Melissa wasn't surprised, but it didn't hurt less.

Instead of staying home and thinking about everything going wrong in her life, Melissa decided it would be a good idea to get out. Her plans for Sunday had no doubt gotten cancelled. Annabelle wouldn't want anything to do with her now. That didn't mean Melissa couldn't explore on her own.

Packing a small bag full of bottles of water, trail mix and granola bars, she was excited to see the state park.

The last thing she grabbed was the map she'd printed off at work.

Brookside sat beside one of the most private and rarely visited areas. Was the land having been settled by shifters the reason it was still pristine? Humans hadn't made their mark on the forest. The trees remained tall and full. Nature could be an awesome thing.

She exited through the back and locked the door behind her.

Melissa had seen the trail through town. She had to keep her pace steady instead of racing down and disappearing between the trees. She craved the peace and solitude she was hoping to find.

There was no one around as she made her way down the dirt path.

Later, when Melissa was more familiar with the area, she'd venture away from where everyone else walked. She'd been hiking for years and knew how to take care of herself. She'd even learned to mark her way with chalk lines on trees.

Trent had always enjoyed hiking with her. Back when they'd first started dating, they'd often taken weekend trips to the mountains.

Melissa hadn't known when she'd begun to get romantically involved with him that Trent was a shifter. Looking back, there had been signs he was different. Until the shifters had decided to go public, though, she'd never expected someday he'd confess he wasn't fully human.

That conversation had been the first strain on their relationship.

Trent had been nervous when he'd invited her over to his apartment to talk. Melissa had foolishly thought he'd wanted to take their relationship to the next level. Maybe move in together. Instead he'd told her he was one of the shifters who were all over the news. He'd told her he could transform into a hyena.

Melissa had been shocked but intrigued. To be able to change into an animal had to be cool.

She'd been an animal lover her entire life, but dating a shifter was a different story. Melissa also wondered if he would have ever told her if the shifters hadn't decided to become public. So, she'd listened to Trent as he explained what made him different, but also how he was still the same man.

Because she'd already been in love with him, Melissa had responded with kind words and acceptance. Had tried to say everything he needed to hear. When Trent had taken her to bed that night, they'd thought things had been settled. Melissa had believed she would be able to come to terms with the secret he'd revealed.

She'd lied to them both.

Melissa hadn't accepted Trent. In the back of her mind, she'd been freaked out. Of course, she hadn't known that until the shit had hit the fan.

Trent had offered her everything he was. He'd been willing to answer any question and even offered to show her his animal. She hadn't wanted to see it. Had never asked. She regretted that now.

Either being older or seeing how much prejudice the shifters had to endure had changed her mind. Hell, it had changed her life. Had changed the way she looked at the world. Melissa wasn't the same person she had been. She didn't know how to prove that to Trent, though. If he never gave her the opportunity to show him the new person she was, Melissa was stuck.

Just stuck.

But if Melissa was going to be stuck somewhere, this was a beautiful piece of America. The canopy above her head, made up of branches and leaves, hid the afternoon sun. It was chillier, but in her pants and long-sleeved T-shirt she was comfortable.

She came to the place where the path split.

Melissa had marked the trail on the right. That would lead her down a short hike before circling back to town. That was the way she'd planned to go. It would take thirty minutes. She wasn't ready to go back to civilization, though. Melissa headed left.

According to the map, she'd have a steep climb in front of her before she reached water.

Excitement raced through her as she hiked and sweat rolled down her back as she continued her trek.

It would have been nice if she had someone to share this perfect hike with. Even Annabelle would have been good company. Not that Annabelle would be her friend now, with Melissa's past with Trent known.

There were other people Melissa might befriend, though.

She hoped she hadn't taken on more than she could handle. Melissa knew if given the opportunity, she'd be a good addition to the Brookside Sheriff Department. All she needed was a chance.

"It's pretty, huh?"

"Oh, my God!" Melissa said. She whirled around. "Annabelle! You scared me."

Annabelle held up her hands. "Sorry."

"What are you doing here?"

"I followed you."

Melissa frowned. "You followed me?" *What the hell? Is this Annabelle's idea of a joke?*

"Don't be mad," Annabelle told her.

"I'm not sure what to feel. Why did you follow me?"

"I was headed to your house to talk to you," Annabelle said. "I saw you leave and decided to see where you were going."

Unbelievable. "That's not creepy at all." She hoped her sarcasm was thick enough for Annabelle to know she was pissed.

Annabelle shrugged. "I was curious."

Melissa pressed her lips together.

"This is where you should say 'curiosity killed the cat'."

Melissa laughed. She couldn't help it.

"And you have good instincts," Annabelle said. "This is my favorite spot in the whole world. Well, after my tree by the back of the bar."

"It's amazing," Melissa agreed. "So, you come here often?"

"No," Annabelle replied. "Not as often as I used to. Logan doesn't like me coming out here all alone."

It wasn't safe. That was why Melissa had been offered the job in the first place. Logan had to worry about Annabelle walking to this gorgeous spot, which wasn't fair.

Annabelle pulled her arm. "Let's get closer."

Melissa let Annabelle lead her to the amazing crystal-clear water. She dropped down to her knees and trailed her fingers over the surface. "It's cold."

"The water in this creek comes from the snow at the top of the mountains."

"Is that why it's so clear?" Melissa asked.

"Yes, it's pure. I used to shift around here and drink from it."

"The grass around it is so green. How'd you even find this place?"

"I got lost."

"You got lost?" Melissa repeated.

"I did. It was a few weeks after I got here. Mac used to let me go out at night, but I was supposed to stay close to the bar. I, of course, didn't listen and kept venturing farther and farther away."

Melissa sat. The soil was moist and smelled good. Annabelle dropped down beside her.

"I bet Mac was pissed," Melissa said.

"Oh, he was. I was only supposed to be gone an hour or so, but by the time I realized I'd gone off course, it was too late." She pointed. "I fell asleep right up there."

"You can sleep in a tree?" Melissa squinted. "That high?"

"I love it. Logan hates heights, so even he can't join me. It's nice and peaceful." Annabelle nudged her. "Feel like a climb?"

"No way in hell." Melissa was not fond of heights, either.

"Figures." Annabelle pouted. "I need to make friends with a bird shifter."

"Not a lot of those around here?" Melissa asked.

"Not that I've met."

"So, what happened next?"

Annabelle giggled. "Mac came barreling through the trees in his bear form. He was massive and angry... Oh, yeah. I was too scared to come down."

Melissa stiffened. "Did he hurt you?"

"Mac?" Annabelle shook her head. "Never. But he gave me the longest lecture of my life."

"Sounds like a good guy."

"Mac is the best. It scares him when something is out of his control. That night, he'd been terrified I'd been hurt and was calling for help."

"So, he's protective?" Melissa asked.

"Maybe a little too protective. He puts everyone else ahead of himself."

"What's going on at the bar?" Melissa questioned.

"Good try." Annabelle leaned into her.

"Hello, ladies."

Melissa turned and spotted a park ranger standing on the trail. It was Garth Stevenson, one of the rangers Magnus didn't trust. He was human as well. "Afternoon." Melissa didn't like the guy.

"Deputy Bishop." He nodded. "And friend."

"Sir," Annabelle said. She didn't offer her name. Melissa noticed how Annabelle shrank away.

"It's beautiful here, isn't it?" Ranger Stevenson asked.

Melissa stood. She wasn't going to let this guy stand over her. Melissa reached down and helped Annabelle to her feet. "We're enjoying it." She made certain to look the ranger in the eye.

"Not many people know about this place," Stevenson stated. "It's not on most of the maps."

"We know about it," Melissa said. She'd gotten her map from Magnus' personal collection. He'd allowed her to print it off to do her exploring.

"I see that." Stevenson looked around. "You ladies be careful. The trails around here can be dangerous if you're not experienced."

"Good thing we have plenty of experience," Melissa responded.

"Ladies." Stevenson dipped his head before leaving them.

It wasn't until Stevenson was out of sight that Melissa realized Annabelle had a death grip on her arm.

"Annabelle? You okay?"

"Sure, why?"

"Because you're about to break my arm."

"Oh, sorry!" Annabelle released her.

Melissa turned to her. "What is it?"

"I don't like him."

"Wait? You know Ranger Stevenson?" Melissa didn't think the rangers went into Brookside unless it was to meet with Magnus.

"I didn't know his name, but I've seen him around."

"Where?"

"Around." Annabelle shrugged.

"I don't like him, either," Melissa confided.

Annabelle peered at her with her dark eyes. She looked vulnerable in that moment, even though Melissa knew Annabelle wasn't. "No?"

"No." Melissa tugged on Annabelle's arm. "Let's get back. We'll walk together this time. I don't want anything to happen to you as you stalk behind me."

Annabelle laughed. "Fine, but whatever will we talk about on the hike back down?"

"You could tell me how you know the ranger. I want to look into this guy further."

"There's nothing to tell." Annabelle glanced behind her. "Really, I've only seen him around."

"Fine." Melissa would get to the bottom of whatever was going on. *Shit, Brookside has more secrets than the LAPD.* Hopefully, those secrets were protecting everyone and not doing harm. "I really did like it here."

Annabelle smiled. "Maybe we can come again."

"I'd like to," she agreed. Melissa glanced at in the direction the ranger had gone. She heard an ATV. *So that's how the ranger got up there. But why didn't I hear him walking up? Why didn't Annabelle?*

She needed to do her research and talk to Magnus.

It was time to get Annabelle back into the safety of the bar. Melissa knew she was taking a chance of running into Trent, but she couldn't let Annabelle walk around unprotected either.

Trent stepped out of The Den and let the front door slam behind him. He'd spotted Annabelle and Melissa on the camera, talking in the parking lot, and decided to see if they were okay.

He didn't know why they were hanging out or how he felt about it. Annabelle was like a little sister to him, but he had a past with Melissa. He'd told Annabelle he didn't want her to hate Melissa, but he kind of did. He wanted Annabelle on his side.

Which was childish and stupid. He was a grown-ass man. Instead of accepting how things were, Trent wanted to throw a fit. He also wanted to have her say she was sorry again, but this time open his arms and accept her apology.

Melissa wasn't going to go away. Having her in front of the bar talking to Annabelle was proof of that. He needed to deal with this shit, now.

"So, you'll let me know what you find out?" Annabelle was asking.

"Uh…"

"Oh, come on!" Annabelle said. "I'm dating a Coalition agent."

"Then maybe I should tell your boyfriend."

Annabelle laughed. "Go ahead." They turned as Trent walked over. "Hey, Trent."

"Hi." He glanced between the two women. Something was going on.

Melissa was already stepping backward. "I'll see you later, Annabelle."

"No! Come in for a drink. It's the least I can do for you insisting on walking me home."

"I got some work to do," Melissa stated. "But I'll see you later."

"Next Sunday, right?"

"Yeah." Melissa turned. "Bye."

"Melissa, wait," Trent called.

"I'll go get ready to open," Annabelle said. She waved her hand, but she was grinning at him. Trent rolled his eyes. *Really?* Did she think he was going to sweep Melissa off her feet and get over the past? *Probably.* Annabelle had turned into a bit of a romantic since she'd started dating Logan.

Melissa turned back around but remained several feet from him.

"What are you looking into?" he asked.

"What?"

"I heard Annabelle ask you if you'd let her know what you find," Trent said. "What are you looking into?"

"I... This is business of the sheriff's department," Melissa said.

He stalked forward. "I'm not going to ask you again."

She straightened her shoulders and glared. "I don't work for you, Trent. I don't answer to you. This is an investigation."

"If this has to do with Annabelle, it concerns me," Trent said. Damn, he didn't mean to sound like an asshole, but he didn't know how to handle all the feelings inside him.

Melissa laughed. "You'll have to stand in line to protect her."

"I know. But no one else is out here right now."

She turned. Like she was going to walk away from him. Or he was pushing her away. Which of course was what he was doing. By making her angry, she wouldn't look at him with that sad, lost expression. "I only wanted to make sure Annabelle got back safely."

"Why do you care?" he asked quietly.

"Because." She whirled around. "Annabelle was nice. Is nice."

"She is," Trent agreed. He had to take a few deep breaths. It was smarter to get Melissa on his side. He'd have to remain strong. "Will you just tell me if she's in danger? I don't like how she keeps getting targeted by the hunters."

She bit her bottom lip while peering around. Trent knew that move.

"There is something," Trent pressed.

"Do you know a park ranger by the name of Garth Stevenson?"

"No. Should I?"

"I don't know."

"Tell me what is going on," Trent said. "Magnus was here earlier updating us on the current investigation. He mentioned that he didn't trust the rangers. I'm guessing he's one of them?"

"Magnus told you? Why?"

"Because whatever is going on is happening in our backyard. Literally. And, like I said, Annabelle seems to be around during the attacks."

"So, the sheriff thinks you guys are targets?" she asked.

"Maybe. It's well-known that this town is full of shifters. Our place is the closest to the forest. We actually own several acres."

"Okay, I get it."

"So, you can tell me what's going on and I can help, or I can give Magnus a call," Trent said.

"You're threatening to call my boss? That's a low blow."

"I'm not sorry," Trent told her.

"I didn't expect you to be." She laughed. "God, you're still an asshole."

"I am. So tell me."

She blew out a breath.

"I'll buy you a beer," Trent offered.

"Oh, really?" Melissa responded. "I thought I was supposed to stay away from you."

"I'm asking you, not the other way around." Although she was right. He was breaking his own rules. "Come on."

"Fine, but if I get into trouble—"

"You won't." Trent motioned toward the bar. "After you."

She sauntered forward. Trent wasn't even a little ashamed as he watched her ass as she walked. *Damn, the hiking shorts are tight.*

"I know you're checking me out," she said without looking back.

He chuckled. "I have no idea what you're talking about."

Melissa yanked open the door. Trent caught it behind her before it could slam shut. The music was already playing. He followed behind, but when she paused in the doorway, he placed his hand on her lower back. It was a familiar gesture.

"In the corner," he said. "That's where we always sit." Trent guided her to the table.

"You stayed!" Annabelle called. She sounded happy. Annabelle didn't connect with other people, usually.

Even though the residents of Brookside loved her, Annabelle kept herself separate. It was just hard for her to trust. But she needed more friends. However, Trent's doubts on trusting Melissa pulled him in opposite directions.

"Two beers," Trent called.

"You got it," Annabelle replied.

"Here, sit." He pulled out a chair before sitting next to her. Trent waited until Annabelle had dropped off two cold bottles to the table before leaning in to Melissa. "Talk."

"I used to enjoy your dominant side," she said. "Not so much anymore."

"I'm waiting," he said.

"I went on a hike into the state park today."

"Okay," he said.

"I didn't realize I was being followed."

Trent frowned. *A park ranger followed her?* That was crossing a line. He'd made sure she was safe the previous night, but it seemed to him Melissa needed a fucking keeper.

"Annabelle saw me leave my house and decided to see what I was up to."

"Wait!" Trent lifted a hand. "Annabelle followed you?"

She held up her beer. "She did."

Trent laughed. Well, he shouldn't be surprised. He never should have doubted where Annabelle's loyalties lay. If Annabelle thought Melissa had wronged him, then she would do whatever she could to ensure Trent wasn't hurt again.

"I'm glad you think it's funny." She glared.

"It kind of is. She doesn't mean any harm," he said.

"I know she doesn't." Melissa took a long pull of her beer.

"She gets a little—"

"Nosy," Melissa stated. "She's nosy."

"Yeah," he agreed.

"But it turned out to be hard not to like her," Melissa said.

"I know. Trust me, I know."

"So, anyway, I ended up at one of Annabelle's favorite spots and we were talking when we ran into one of the rangers."

"Garth Stevenson?"

"Yes," she replied. "It was weird him showing up where we were. He even mentioned the site wasn't on all of the maps."

"You were at the creek," he guessed.

Melissa nodded. "While he was there, Annabelle was very tense. She said she didn't like him."

"I didn't think she knew any of the rangers."

"She told me she'd seen him around," Melissa said. "I got a really bad feeling about him. He creeped me out."

"What else?"

"I'm pretty sure he threatened us," Melissa whispered. She lifted the bottle to take a long pull.

"He threatened you?" He fisted his hand under the table.

"Told us to be careful. That the trails were dangerous."

"Could have just been a friendly warning."

"No, it wasn't."

"So, what're you going to do?" he asked.

"I'm going to do my job," she said. "In a day, I'll know everything there is to know about him."

"I can help," he offered. With Mac running an underground network to help relocate shifters who needed a safe place, they had one of the best hackers in the world. Carter could get into any database.

"How?" Suspicion coated her tone.

"I might not be a cop anymore, but I have connections."

"I work for one of your connections," she reminded him.

Trent grinned.

"You want me to share, but you're not going to give me anything?" she scoffed. "How's that fair?"

"Because it's not my story to share," Trent said.

"This has to do with the bar?"

"What do you know about it?" he asked. There was no way Annabelle would tell anyone anything about what went on downstairs from the bar.

"Nothing," she said. "It's all real hush-hush."

He leaned back.

"Thank you for the offer," she told him. "I can handle it."

"Fine." He drained the rest of the beer.

"At least keep an eye on Annabelle when she's here. I'll let Logan know as well."

"We will."

Melissa stood. "Thanks for the beer, Trent."

"Oh, come on," he drawled. "Don't be mad."

She planted her palms on the table right in front of him. "I didn't think you'd tell me anything. I was hoping, but I knew you wouldn't. The only reason I told you is because I figure Magnus would, anyway. And I want you to keep an eye on Annabelle."

He leaned forward. "Then why're you mad?"

"I'm not mad," she said. "Just disappointed." Melissa walked away.

This time, he didn't watch her go. His instincts were screaming at him to follow her and not let her out of his sight.

"You still like her," Annabelle said, dropping into the chair Melissa had vacated.

Trent groaned.

"I can tell."

"It's in the past," he responded. He was not having *that* conversation.

"Are you sure? The way she looks at you tells me she isn't over you any more than you are her."

He narrowed his eyes. "What'd you tell her?"

"You mean, did I tell her about all the women you pick up here?"

Trent set his bottle down, hard. "You didn't."

"What, you want me to lie to my new friend?"

"Annabelle."

"Oh, look, Logan's here!" She jumped up.

Trent tried to grab her, but she wiggled away and raced across the floor.

"Save me!" She threw herself at Logan. "Trent's going to get me."

Logan laughed then picked her up. He started to carry her back to Trent.

"What're you doing?" she cried. "He threatened to spank me."

Trent nearly spat out the drink he'd just taken.

Logan stumbled. "What?"

"I did not," Trent defended. "But I think you should."

"She'd like it too much," Logan complained. He sat next to Logan with Annabelle in his lap. "What'd she do?"

"I can't tell if she's screwing with me or not," Trent confessed.

"About?" Logan asked.

"I'm not screwing with you," Annabelle said.

"And what did you tell her?" Trent pressed.

"Nothing," Annabelle said. "By some unspoken rule neither one of us brought your name up."

Trent ignored the disappointed crawling up his spine.

"You haven't seen anyone serious since you've got here," Annabelle told him. "Why is that, exactly? You know, in case my new friend asks."

"Maybe you should stay out of it," Logan advised.

Annabelle snorted. "Yeah right." She glared at Trent. "Like Trent stays out of my business."

Trent tipped his beer. "Logan's still standing, isn't he?"

Logan frowned. "How'd I get drawn into this?"

"Because you love me," Annabelle replied.

"I'd love you more if you got me a beer," Logan said.

"Fine." Annabelle stood.

"I do love her, but she drives me crazy," Logan whispered.

Trent chuckled. "I know what you mean."

More patrons came in, so Annabelle became busy. On her way past to another table, she dropped off Logan's beer and a second for Trent.

"Any progress from the hunter arrested last night?" Trent asked.

"Claims he was all alone, although Magnus and Mac smelled a second guy."

"So, he's already lying," Trent stated. "Anything else?"

"Not yet," Logan said. "I'm letting him sweat it out in lock up. Dude's got a clean record, not even a speeding ticket. I told him he'd be going into Coalition custody and he freaked. I think I can use that."

"I hope so."

"I will," Logan said. "I'm getting tired of this fucking game. Annabelle keeps getting caught in the middle and eventually her luck will run out."

"Have you talked her into staying away from the forest?"

Logan snorted. "I tried. Mac tried. Magnus even tried."

Trent wasn't surprised Annabelle refused to listen. She was too set on not giving up her freedoms. Shifting and climbing her trees was the one thing Annabelle had to do every single day. Unlike the rest of them, Annabelle had a need to shift.

"I couldn't even keep her from hiking today."

That reminded Trent of what Melissa had said earlier. "Have you spoken to Melissa?"

"Melissa? No, why?"

"The girls ran into a ranger today. From talking to Melissa, she seemed disturbed."

"You talked to Melissa?" Logan questioned. "After telling her to stay away from you?"

"I heard Annabelle and her talking. I was curious."

"Who's the ranger?" Logan asked.

"Garth Stevenson," Trent said.

"I've met him a few times."

"In town?" Trent leaned closer.

Logan frowned. "At the station. We've had all the employees of the state park here to interview them. Magnus thinks at least one of them is involved."

"I know. Magnus told us earlier. But what I'm asking is if you've seen him in town? Other than the station."

"No."

"You need to get Annabelle to talk to you about today. Melissa told me Annabelle was really bothered. I think she knows more than she's telling us," Trent said.

"Annabelle wouldn't hold anything back from us," Logan stated.

"I know. But I think it might not be something she's even aware of. She's not a cop. She doesn't think like us. If anyone can walk her through her feelings, it'll be you, though."

"I can try," Logan responded.

"Good."

"What're you going to do?" Logan asked.

"I'm going to have Carter look into him."

"You know we're doing that at our office, right?"

Trent grinned. "But we have Carter."

"I know you do," Logan said. "Go ahead. Let me know what you find out, please. It's still our investigation."

"I'm trying to help."

"I bet." Logan nodded toward Annabelle. "We give your group a lot of room to maneuver because of the good you do here. But that's only going to go so far when we're dealing with an actual case which will have to go to court. I have superiors, you know."

"I'm not going to mess up anything for you," Trent told him.

"Keep me informed."

Trent rose. "I'll talk to you later." He patted Logan on the shoulder as he walked behind him. "I'm going to see Carter now."

"Later," Logan called.

Trent strolled out of the main bar into the private hallway. He kept walking until he got to the end of the hall. With a glance over his shoulder, he confirmed he was alone before he pressed his hand to the reader. They took precautions to ensure no one unauthorized could get downstairs.

The custom addition was rarely seen by anyone outside their own group. Logan hadn't even been down there.

The *click* of the hidden door opening echoed in the narrow hall.

Trent pushed the entry the rest of the way open before stepping through. He then pushed the door closed behind him.

"Hey, Trent."

"Carter," Trent called as he walked down the steps. "What's up?"

"You didn't even bring me anything to eat," Carter said. He turned in his chair and grinned. "I thought you loved me."

"Hungry?" Trent taunted. "I heard Kelly is working on a roast."

"You're mean," Carter complained.

"I know. But if you do me a favor, I might bring you a really big plate," Trent told him. "Because I do love you." He walked up beside Carter. The little deer shifter had six monitors in front of him, all with different stuff on the screens. Trent didn't have a clue what any of it meant.

"What do you want?" Carter asked.

"I need you to find out everything you can on someone," Trent requested. "I mean everything."

Carter laughed. "I've been waiting for this." He opened the bottom drawer of his desk and pulled out a manila folder. He handed it to Trent. "I haven't shown this to anyone else."

Confused but willing to play along, Trent opened up the file. The first thing he saw was the official photo from Melissa's LAPD days. "What's this?"

"That is everything there is on your girl. From her first day of school to the week before she arrived here. I figured I'd stay out of the sheriff's records. For now."

Trent snorted. "Not like you haven't poked in there before."

"I plead the fifth," Carter replied.

He snapped the folder closed. "I don't need this."

Carter frowned. "I thought —"

"I know everything I need to about Melissa." He threw the file down on Carter's desk.

"I don't think you do," Carter spun his chair to him before he rose. "Take my word, you need to read what's in there." He picked back up the manila file.

"Fine." Trent grabbed it before sticking it under his arm. "Now, if you want to earn your dinner, I need my favor."

"I could call Kelly myself. Or Annabelle. They like me more, anyway."

"No one likes you more than me." Trent pinched Carter's cheek. "Please."

With a heavy sigh, Carter dropped into his chair. "What do you need?"

"Park ranger, Garth Stevenson," Trent supplied.

"Ohhhh." Carter rubbed his hands together. "I'm going to enjoy this."

"How long do you think it's going to take?"

"A couple of hours to get the surface stuff and at least a day for the rest."

"Good enough," Trent said. "I'll make sure you get a plate as soon as it's ready." He turned and walked off.

"Trent?"

He stopped. "Yeah?"

"Read it," Carter told him. Then he bent over his keyboard and started to type.

Trent didn't respond. He wasn't going to promise anything. He strolled up the stairs. As he walked down the hall, Kelly was heading toward him. "That for Carter?" he asked, nodding to the plate of food.

"Yep," she replied. "If I don't take it to him, he'll starve before leaving his cave."

"Will you tell him I asked you to bring it down?" he requested.

Kelly laughed. "Trying to earn favors?"

"Always." He passed by, continuing to his room.

Once inside, Trent threw the folder onto his mattress before stomping over to the mini-fridge. It was only big enough to hold a couple of cans of beer and some bottles of water, but it was enough for him. There was no way he was going to spy on his ex-girlfriend without a beer. And he didn't want to go back to the bar floor where he'd have to watch Logan and Annabelle being in love. Not that he was jealous, He wasn't, not really.

He grabbed a can of beer then plopped down on the bed. Adjusting the pillows behind him, Trent stared at his boots. The file lay right next to them. If he opened this door, he wouldn't be able to go back.

Carter was the best at ferreting out all kinds of information.

Trent was only now able to look at Melissa without anger taking over. If he saw what she'd been up to for the last several years, would Trent be able to look her in the eye again? He just didn't know the answer to that question. But he didn't like being in the dark about things, either.

Fuck, now that he had the damn folder, he had to look.

He leaned forward and snagged the file then popped open his beer. It looked like he had a long night of reading ahead of him. Trent skimmed over the early years of Melissa's life. He already knew most of it, anyway, from when they'd been dating. He couldn't look at the section that covered his partner's death, though. Carter had included a copy of the report Trent had filed. The connection Carter had found was weak. There'd been phone calls from Melissa's apartment to Adam's cell phone. Of course. Trent knew he'd made those calls.

The LAPD investigation into Adam's death had been a joke, even tying Melissa and Adam together. Like they were having an affair, even though Adam was married. There was no mention of Trent at all. *What a crock of shit.* Everyone knew about him and Melissa. Before he'd come out as a shifter, they'd been open about their relationship.

She'd been transferred to a new department not long after he'd left. That was where he started to read. Just the first few paragraphs in, he knew he was going to need more beer.

It was both better and worse than he'd expected.

Trent was proud of Melissa but ashamed of himself.

No wonder Magnus had hired her. She'd been all up in the LAPD bosses' faces about the treatment of shifters until she left to move to Brookside.

He'd underestimated her.

Damn, he needed more than a beer. A couple of shots or a bottle might do the trick.

Chapter Five

Grant Stevenson should not have been working for a federal agency or anywhere near law enforcement. *How in the hell did he get the job?* The guy had had numerous complaints made against him, but they'd all been dropped.

The complaints, made by shifters, had increased in the past year.

Melissa knew in her gut there was something wrong with Grant. Now she needed to put all the pieces together. Magnus had every reason to be suspicious.

"I brought you a coffee."

She glanced up at where Logan was leaning over her desk. "What?"

Logan held up a Styrofoam cup. "Coffee?"

"Oh, God, yes!" She reached for the cup.

He pulled it back. "Whatcha working on?"

"I'll tell you if you give me the coffee," she retorted.

Logan handed her the coffee.

Melissa took a sip before sighing. "I needed that."

"Grant Stevenson," Logan stated. "Tell me what you've found."

She lifted an eyebrow.

"I talked to Trent last night. Then find you in the office before anyone else. I can put two and two together."

"This guy is something else," Melissa told him.

"I don't disagree," Logan said.

"Did Annabelle say anything about him?" she asked. There had to be more than the guy giving Annabelle the creeps. Melissa wished she was closer to Annabelle to get some answers.

"I haven't asked her yet," Logan said. "I wanted to find out what I could on my own first. I don't want her involved in this investigation."

Melissa smiled. "Please let me be in the room when you tell her."

Logan snorted. "I won't put it in those words. I'm not stupid."

Melissa nodded as she drank more coffee. "Look at this." She pushed a paper she'd printed out earlier. It showed all the cases in which Grant's name had been mentioned. Even though nothing had gone to court, the digital age made record-keeping so much better.

"Shit." Logan sat on the edge of her desk.

"He doesn't like shifters," Melissa said. "I'm trying to go back further to see where this hatred comes from. I'm not getting anywhere, though. There are some closed files that have to do with his family. I think it's his brother. A judge ordered them sealed, however. Which is weird, because his brother isn't a minor."

"Political?"

"Maybe."

Logan glanced toward the back, where the holding cells were located. "Have you checked on our prisoner?"

"No." Melissa shook her head. "James was still here when I arrived. I offered to man the phones so he could take off. He checked on Bono just before he left."

"I'm going to question him this morning before I have Fabian and Fredrick transfer him to the Coalition custody. He hasn't said one word, but I'm remaining hopeful."

"I hope you can get something from him," Melissa said. "I wonder if it was Stevenson who Magnus followed the other night."

"I don't think so," Logan said. "Magnus would have recognized his scent."

"Oh, I didn't think about that," Melissa admitted. "It's so cool everything you guys can do."

Logan chuckled. "It helps, although we're having trouble getting the courts to recognize our abilities. Saying you knew who the perp was because of his scent is controversial."

"I bet," Melissa commented. "Still, it narrows down the suspect list."

"It does." Logan rose. "I'd better get to work. You'll let me know whatever else you find?"

"Of course," she agreed.

He started to walk away but paused. "I wanted to say thanks."

She turned her chair around. "For?"

"Looking out for Annabelle. She'll be the first one to tell you she can take care of herself, and she can, but she doesn't always think before she acts."

"Annabelle is great. I don't want anything to happen to her or anyone else around here. Magnus brought me in to keep everyone safe, and that's what I'm going to do."

Logan grinned. "So, anyway, thanks." He walked away before she could respond.

Feeling better than she had in a couple of days, Melissa turned back to her research.

She ran through Grant's associates and family. Maybe there was a connection there with a shifter somewhere. Scrolling through the information she found, Melissa started the painstaking task of trying to figure out Grant's ultimate plan. Melissa was sure Grant was responsible for what was happening in Brookside.

The phone on the desk rang and she picked up the receiver. "Sheriff's office," she answered.

"Who's this?" the male voice on the other end demanded.

Melissa rolled her eyes, but had to remain professional. "This is Deputy Bishop. Can I help you?"

"You're the new one? The human?"

"Yes, sir, but I'm an experienced officer. Did you need some help?"

The man huffed. "This is Lewis Grainger. Someone has been trespassing on my land. I want the sheriff here."

"Yes, Mr. Grainger. Can I get your address?"

He growled. "The sheriff knows where it is!"

"I understand, sir. If I could have it for my report, please? I'll make a report and call Sheriff Magnus. Will that work?"

"Fine. It's 211 Fairgrounds Road."

"And have you seen anyone?"

"No, just footprints and the scent of someone I don't know. I want this investigated. I know there is something fishy going on."

"Yes, sir. I'll get someone over there shortly."

Mr. Grainger hung up on her.

"Great," Melissa grumbled.

"Problem?" Logan called.

"A resident called and said he's had trespassers on his property. He didn't recognize the scent."

"Where?" Logan asked.

"Two hundred blocks off Fairgrounds Road."

"Call Magnus and tell him we'll meet him there. The Graingers' place is connected to the state park on the other side of town. It may be how the hunters are coming into town," Logan said.

Melissa jumped to her feet while grabbing her cell phone. She made the call even as she scrambled to gather her belongings and shoved them into her bag. Logan was already striding toward the front door. She had to rush to catch up.

Remembering she'd promised to watch the phones, she stopped at Carl's desk and hit the Transfer button before punching in her number. The calls would be redirected to her cell phone.

By the time she got outside, Logan was in his truck, motioning her to join him.

She raced over to the passenger side and yanked open the door. She jumped in, but before she could get the door closed, Logan was already backing up.

"Logan!" she called.

"Sorry!" Logan was speeding down the street. "We've been all over the stretch connected to the state park, but haven't been able to locate where the hunters are coming in. This is our best lead so far."

Melissa could understand why this was so important. If Magnus or Logan recognized the scents, they'd know who was involved. Who couldn't be trusted. "Just don't kill us on the way there."

He slowed down. "Right."

Logan didn't have lights or sirens on his truck, but they still made it across town in a matter of minutes. He did take his foot off the gas when they reached the gates leading up a gravel drive. The gates were open and, as they drove forward, she saw an older man standing out front of the two-story ranch style home, holding a shotgun.

"Is that Grainger?" she asked Logan.

"I hope so," Logan replied. He glanced over at her after stopping in front of the older gentleman. "Or we are going to have bigger problems."

"Well, let's talk to him." She opened the door, but kept her hand by her side where her weapon was in reach.

"Mr. Grainger?" Logan called. He too was standing with his hand on his weapon.

"Who're you?" Mr. Grainger asked. "Where's the sheriff?"

"He's on his way," Melissa said. "I'm Deputy Bishop. I spoke to you on the phone."

Mr. Grainger sniffed. "The human." Then he turned his gaze to Logan. He sniffed again, but this time his eyes narrowed. "Lion?"

"Yes, sir," Logan replied. He pulled out his badge and ID from his breast pocket. "I'm Agent Logan Coldwell with the Shifter Coalition."

"Annabelle's fellow?" Mr. Grainger questioned.

"Yes, sir."

Mr. Grainger lowered the gun. "That's fine, then. Come along and I'll show you the tracks. I don't have all day."

Logan glanced over at her and grinned. Melissa rolled her eyes. Sure. She couldn't be trusted because she was human and Logan being with the Coalition didn't matter. But because Logan was dating Annabelle, they were now deemed acceptable.

The old man didn't wait for them. He strode away.

It was a big place. There was a wooden fenced lining the outer edge of the property, but the fence was only about four feet high. Easy enough for someone to jump over.

"Keep up," Mr. Grainger snapped.

Melissa hurried to catch up. Logan was peering around as she had been.

Once they rounded the house, there were several buildings scattered about. Perfect spots for someone to hide in. Melissa waved her hand to get Logan's attention.

Logan lifted his head and sniffed. Then looked over and shook his head.

She had to trust Logan knew for a fact that no one else was around. Melissa didn't feel comfortable, though, so she unsnapped her holster.

Neither shifter appeared nervous.

It must be nice to have such strong senses. Melissa could've used that enhanced ability when she'd been with the LAPD. Too bad the other cops hadn't learned to utilize the skills the shifters could bring.

Mr. Grainger stopped around some stalls covered in hay but without any animals. Logan and Melissa stepped up on either side of the older shifter.

"There." He pointed.

Melissa tried to see what Mr. Grainger was pointing at. There was nothing there.

"Ah," Logan said. He crouched down. "At least three people."

"The tracks weren't here two nights ago," Mr. Grainger stated. "I just moved the horses out to the pasture so I can fix up the stalls."

"Yeah, they're recent," Logan agreed.

Melissa stepped closer before leaning down beside Logan. She saw the very faint outline of a boot. *Wow, for Mr. Grainger to spot that, he has to have excellent sight even at his age.*

"It's not any of the men who work for me, either," Mr. Grainger said. "The scent is human."

Logan turned his head. "And I recognize one of the scents." He nodded to Melissa.

"Stevenson?" she asked.

"Yep, one of the other scents is familiar, but I can't place it. Not yet."

"Does this have to do with the illegal hunting?" Mr. Grainger demanded.

"Sir..." Melissa stood. "Maybe you should—"

"Don't you try to handle me, little missy. This is my community and I'll protect it." Mr. Grainger lifted the shotgun over his head.

She needed to deal with this situation right or the residents were never going to trust her. Logan started to stand, but Melissa waved him off. If she let Logan stick up for her, then she wouldn't earn Mr. Grainger's respect.

Melissa turned to the older shifter. "Mr. Grainger, you're right—this is your community. It's also mine. I know you're concerned for your family, friends and neighbors. I share that concern as well. I might be human, but I am here to help. I was only going to suggest you go out front and wait for Magnus. He'll be here any minute. He'll want to talk to you to see if you've noticed anything else."

Mr. Grainger nodded. "Of course. I should have thought about that. I'll go wait for the sheriff." He took off and Melissa sighed.

"Nicely done," Logan praised.

"They're never going to accept me," she complained.

"Give it time."

She snorted. "Which is exactly what Magnus says."

"He knows what he's talking about. When I arrived, I was an agent who was sticking my nose where it didn't belong. No one would talk to me. They avoided me whenever I was around even after I started dating Annabelle. Finally, they've opened up and somewhat accepted me. But as you could see from earlier, I'm still not truly trusted."

Okay, he has a point.

"Look at this here." Logan pointed. "The way these footprints are more noticeable here mean they stayed here for a little bit. Maybe someone, Mr. Grainger or one of his men, was around. We'll need to ask."

"I never would have seen these on my own," she admitted. Now that they'd been pointed out to her, she could see the evidence left behind.

"I could smell their sweat," Logan told her. "So, I knew to look around. I can also distinguish that the scents are newer compared to the rest of the stalls. It's not so much as picking them out as knowing that they don't belong."

"Okay." Melissa peered around. "So, three humans come out of the state park and cross Mr. Grainger's property. Someone is walking around, so they run in here. Wait until the coast is clear before moving on."

"The question is, where did they go after leaving here?" Logan responded. "We didn't have any incidents last night."

"Huh." If the unknown humans had been in Brookside, there had to have been a reason. "Maybe nothing's been called in yet?"

"I have Mac checking." Magnus strolled forward without Mr. Grainger.

"Sheriff," Melissa greeted. "You have Mac checking for what?" Why did Mac have so much pull in the town? He wasn't part of the sheriff's department, and yet everyone, including Magnus, appeared to have no problem involving him in an official investigation.

"We have a communication program for the town. Mac makes a call, that person makes a call, until every resident is accounted for. It helps us keep any eye on what is going on inside the town without stepping on people's toes. The residents move here for privacy, so the phone link is utilized during threats. Mac will make sure everyone is aware to look out for strangers."

"Great. Hopefully you won't get a call on me," she replied.

Magnus shook his head. "They already know who you are."

"Magnus, see if you recognize these scents," Logan called over. "I'm going to take Melissa around to check if there's any more evidence."

"Fine." Magnus strode forward. "I have Fredrick taking Mr. Grainger's statement. Fabian and Carl are canvassing the south and east sections of the property, so you two take the north and west."

"Yes, sir," Melissa agreed. She winked at Magnus when he frowned at her. It wasn't her fault she'd been trained to say sir all the time. Magnus didn't like it, but it was a hard habit to break.

"Just get going," Magnus griped at her.

Logan chuckled while leading the way from the stalls. Melissa followed. The property Mr. Grainger owned was very nice. Well-kept and large. The farther north they walked, the more distinct the smell of horses became.

"The horses would have been startled if it had been shifters sneaking around," Logan said. "That would have alerted Mr. Grainger and he'd have met the trespassers with his shotgun."

"He still might," Melissa commented. "If whoever was here returns."

"Good point. I'll keep one of the men close by. Can't have Mr. Grainger shooting anyone we might need to talk to."

"We know Stevenson has been here. Isn't that enough to bring him in for questioning?"

Logan shook his head. "Not yet. They don't know we found out how they're getting into the town. I don't want to blow the first lead we've gotten." He pointed toward a large pasture. "Head in that direction. Look for any signs someone has walked through the grass recently."

"Where are you going?"

"I want to check out a few of the buildings. Plus the horses will spook if I go near them."

Oh, yeah, the shifter thing. Maybe being human does have some advantages. "Sure."

Melissa continued walking along, using her flashlight to help with her vision. She could smell the fresh grass, manure and the heavy odor of animal. She opened a latched gate before making certain it closed behind her.

Two dozen horses stood grazing. She'd never been so close to such large animals. Being from the city hadn't given her a lot of experience with any type of wildlife. *Are horses considered wildlife?* She didn't know. Not that it mattered. She kept her distance, not wanting to upset the gentle creatures.

Just when Melissa though she was wasting her time, she spotted a cigarette butt lying on the ground.

It could be from Mr. Grainger or one of the workers, but it was suspicious since she hadn't noticed any others.

Melissa crouched down where the cigarette butt was lying. There was also the tip of a boot print, probably from when the person stomped out the end. She narrowed her eyes, hoping to see if it was of the same boot as in the stall.

She couldn't tell.

Pulling out her phone, she took a few pictures before standing. She looked up at the state park tree line several yards away. This could be the path that Stevenson and his cronies had taken. Melissa started forward, trying to remain on the same hidden trail they'd have taken.

As she walked farther from the house, the horses picked up their heads to watch her.

It was sort of eerie, the way those big dark eyes followed her movements.

A smaller brown horse, or colt, ambled over on skinny legs. Melissa stopped as the cute little guy nudged her side. She reached out, laying her hand on the magnificent beast's side, feeling each breath the little guy took. *Wow.*

Movement by one of the large trees caught her attention and Melissa realized she was getting off-track. She patted the little colt's side before trying to push him off. He pushed back harder, and Melissa almost fell over.

"Okay," she said. "But I have to get back to work. We don't want the lion to come look for me."

Melissa marched toward her destination, unsure of what she'd seen from the corner of her eye. Probably some animal that didn't want to be around the horses.

The colt stayed by her side as she hiked up the hill. This property was so large she was thinking once again that she needed to up her workout routine. She hadn't done as much walking in the last five years as she'd done in one weekend.

But she felt good.

Melissa glanced over to the colt as he began to dance around. He kicked up his front legs while making some sort of soft sound. Since she didn't speak horse, natural or shifter, she had no idea what was wrong with him.

Maybe he didn't want to go so far from his herd?

She stopped walking. "Well, go back." She motioned with her hand. "Find your mom or dad." Damn, she hoped this was a natural horse, because if it was a shifter, he'd surely think she was nuts talking to a horse. "Go," she said, anyway.

The colt pounded a front hoof into the ground in front of her.

Whatever. She turned her back and the colt took off in the opposite direction.

Guess he doesn't want my company anymore.

Melissa took a step before a boom echoed around her. Fuck, she knew that sound. She looked around to see the horses scattering, making wild cries. Oh, God! Had someone shot a horse? *Shit, the colt.* She turned and heard a second blast.

Pain bloomed in her arm and she glanced down. *Blood.*

Melissa froze. She knew the sight of blood. But on her?

"Get down! Melissa! Get down!" Logan screamed.

She blinked at him as he ran toward her. *Damn, he's fast.*

"Gun!" he yelled.

Finally, the events taking place snapped together. Melissa let her body go limp and crashed gracelessly to the hard floor. Someone had shot at her. *Jesus Christ, I've been shot.* Melissa covered her head with her uninjured arm, hoping to avoid any more bullets. She was out in the open, though. There wasn't any cover around. She couldn't even run for the trees as that was where she suspected the shots were coming from.

There was more yelling around as Logan ran past her. "Stay there. Magnus is right behind me."

That's nice. But she shouldn't be lying down on the job when her boss arrived. Melissa rolled to her injured side so she could pull out her weapon with her right hand. At least she'd been shot in the left.

Her arm was throbbing, but the pain wasn't as bad as she'd expected.

Of course, she'd never been shot before. Hell, she'd never shot anyone else either. Lying back on her stomach, she rested her right arm on the ground while trying to cover the direction Logan had raced off in. She couldn't see him any longer, though.

"Melissa!" Magnus dropped down beside her. "Are you okay? Where are you hit?"

Melissa blinked up at him. She was beginning to feel sick to her stomach. "It doesn't even hurt that bad," she whispered. Shouldn't her arm hurt worse? Was she dying, or something? If she died out here, would Trent know how much she regretted what she'd done? Maybe he'd forgive her? He could start his life over and not worry about her showing back up.

"Melissa. I need you to open your eyes," Magnus ordered.

"Okay." She complied. Magnus was leaning over her. looking worried. "I think I'm okay."

"I'm going to take a look. Just remain still."

"Logan—" She tried to sit up, but Magnus held her down.

"Fabian and Carl went after him. They'll get the shooter."

He moved around to her other side and lifted her arm. She cried out.

"Sorry," he said. "There's a lot of blood."

"It's okay," she slurred. Her arm was going numb, so that had to be good.

Magnus wiped at her arm, which re-woke the pain.

"Ouch!" She tried to pull away, but Magnus held her wrist.

"I think you were grazed. I need to get a better look at your injury, though," Magnus told her. "I'm going to wrap your arm."

He yanked at his uniform shirt, the buttons popping off, then tore off a strip. As he tightened it around her biceps, she grunted.

"Sorry. It has to be tight to stop the bleeding."

"It's fine," she responded.

"Let's get you up." Magnus helped her.

Melissa hissed, her hip aching from her fall.

"Are you hurt somewhere else?" Magnus demanded.

"No," she answered. "I fell."

"On your feet," Magnus said. Melissa didn't even have to move. Magnus picked her up before gently placing her on her feet.

She gripped her injured arm, holding it close to her body.

Magnus ran his hands over her shoulder then down her side. "Just your hip?"

Melissa had to think about the question. Her mind was blurry and she was exhausted. "Yes."

"Okay, do you want to walk or for me to carry you?"

She scoffed. "You are so not carrying me."

"I can," he told her. "I'm strong enough."

"Colt!" She pushed Magnus out of the way while stumbling back to where the horses had gathered into a tight circle. "Colt!" she called.

"What the hell are you doing?" Magnus growled. "Did you hurt your head?"

"No!" she exclaimed. "The baby horse was with me. Did he get shot?"

"There's Grainger." Magnus pointed. "We'll have him look over his herd." He walked over and Melissa leaned against him.

"That's probably a good idea," she said. "I couldn't talk to Colt."

"I'm not sure what you mean, but I think we need to get you to the hospital." Magnus helped her walk across the pasture. *Jeez, how far is the car?* Her leg started to get heavy.

"Hold on," Magnus told her. Then he lifted her into his strong arms.

Melissa laid her head against his wide chest. Magnus's heart was beating against her ear in a soothing rhythm. "You need to calm down," she told her boss.

"I've never had one of my deputies shot before," Magnus said. "It pisses me off."

Melissa giggled. "Me, too."

Magnus grunted. "Relax. We'll get you taken care of."

"Is she all right?" Mr. Grainger had reached them.

"You have to check on Colt," she told the old shifter. "I think he was trying to warn me someone was in the forest. He started to act funny then ran away. I don't know where the first shot landed. I didn't get hit until the second. Colt might be hurt!" She felt bad the little horse might have been injured for merely walking by her.

"I'll check him out," Mr. Grainger said. "I can see him over with his mom, so I think he's okay."

"You know what she's talking about?" Magnus demanded.

Mr. Grainger winked at her and she had to grin back. Yeah, he knew. The colt would be okay.

Chapter Six

Trent stomped up the steps to Melissa's house and banged on her front door. He leaned close so he could hear if there was any movement inside. *There, a shuffling sound.* He pounded again.

"Jeez, I'm coming," he heard her muttering.

For the first time since he'd found out she'd been attacked, he started to breathe normally. He'd wanted to come to her as soon as he'd learned about what had happened out at the Grainger place, but Mac had needed him to secure the bar and some of the other houses in town. They were going into lockdown since Logan hadn't managed to catch up to the shooter.

The front door opened and Melissa peered out at him. She frowned, which made him want to grin. Instead he went with his instinct. "Are you okay?" he demanded. Trent pushed his way inside, making her back up. Her arm was in a sling and she had dark circles under her eyes.

"Huh?"

Trent caught her free hand. He held her in place while peering down at her. Her eyes were dazed. He grinned this time. "Painkillers?"

"Yeeeaaaaah."

Chuckling, he led her over to the couch, where it appeared she'd been camped out. There were a couple of pillows and a large flannel blanket as well as bottles of water on the coffee table.

"You need to sit back down," he told her. She wasn't steady on her feet. He helped her climb back on the couch and she hissed.

"What?" he asked.

"Hip. Fell. It hurts."

He growled, unable to keep it in. She could have been killed. He was so furious. If the fucking shooter had been in front of him, he'd have torn the guy apart with his teeth. "Okay, just lie back. Is there anything you need?"

"No, I'm fine." She looked around her living room. "I was watching a movie?"

He glanced at the screen. She'd paused the television in the middle of a familiar comedy. He picked up the remote and pressed Play.

She moaned as she settled back against the pillows.

Trent picked up the blanket and wrapped it around her shoulders. She looked so delicate bundled up there. He brushed the hair from her face. "Have you eaten?"

She squinted.

"I'll take that as a no," he answered himself. "Stay here." Trent rose and strolled out of the living room.

The layout of the house was pretty simple. The living room exited into a narrow hall then led to the kitchen. Her kitchen was clean and had modern appliances. He opened up the fridge. He grabbed the bottle of orange juice and poured her a glass, which he found in a nearby cabinet. Then he opened the pantry.

She had soup and crackers. That would have to do. Trent couldn't do much more than make soup or sandwiches. He grabbed a pan before dumping in a can of tomato soup and warming it up. Then he began making a grilled cheese sandwich.

It took less than ten minutes to get everything prepared and the kitchen cleaned up. He didn't want to leave a mess for her to have to deal with.

He carried the plate and bowl to the living room.

Melissa was still curled into a tight ball on the couch. She looked up at him as he entered the room.

"I made you something to eat," he said. Trent sat down next to her and handed her the plate.

She had to reach across herself to take it with her uninjured arm. "Thanks."

"Let me help you," he said.

"Why are you here?" Her voice was soft as she spoke.

Trent froze while reaching to take the plate back. He sighed but knew she had every reason to question his motives. She didn't know he'd read the file Carter had given him.

The woman who now sat next to him bruised and hurt had taken the mission of cleaning up the LAPD. When he'd read what she'd done to their former officers, he'd been both shocked and pleased. After he'd left the LAPD, she'd kept her head down and out of trouble for a couple of months. Then, in an almost sudden change, she'd began questioning superiors, challenging the way shifter suspects were treated and basically being a pain in the ass.

Damn, she had changed, and not just since she'd arrived in Brookside.

Which made him question himself and how he'd walked away from the LAPD.

It should have been him taking on the bigoted assholes inside the department. Instead Melissa had attempted to right the wrongs that had been responsible for Adam's death and other horrible acts against shifters.

"Trent?" She nudged his side.

"Sorry." He swallowed hard then sat back. "When I heard what had happened, I realized that by holding a grudge, I wasn't doing either of us any favors."

"When I thought I'd been shot, I wondered if you'd ever forgive me."

"You were shot," he snarled.

"Actually, I was grazed. It wasn't that bad."

"You could have been killed!" he declared.

"But I wasn't," she said. "I'll be back to work in a few days."

Trent didn't even want to think about her returning to the investigation that had made her a target in the first place. "Let's not talk about that now," he said. "You need to eat and rest."

She smiled. "So, we're going to be friends now?"

Trent didn't think so. With what he'd found out about Melissa, he couldn't see himself being around her and not wanting to be with her. "Yes, we're going to be friends."

"Okay." She began to eat her sandwich. She had trouble eating the soup, but he helped her.

The comedy played on the television and they watched it while she ate. Trent laid the plates on the coffee table then leaned back. He slung his arm over the back of the couch while stretching his legs out in front of him. Mac knew where he was and Trent didn't plan on leaving anytime soon.

Magnus said that all the deputies were on duty and would do drive-bys, checking on Melissa, but Trent didn't want her to be alone. It had taken Logan roping Annabelle in to help him to allow Trent to come over to Melissa's alone. Annabelle had wanted to come with her. But Trent wanted some time for the two of them.

The movie ended and Melissa pointed at the remote.

"You can find something else to watch," she said.

As he thumbed through the menu, Melissa leaned against his side.

Trent let his arm fall onto her shoulder as she cuddled to him. They used to watch TV like this all the time. Maybe it was the painkillers she was on that had her getting close, but he didn't care. He'd wanted to hold her since he'd first arrived.

He found a new action movie that he hadn't seen and settled on it.

"I missed this one in the theaters," she said. Melissa yawned and he held her tighter.

"Me, too," he said. Of course, Brookside didn't have a movie theater, so he'd have to go out of town to visit one. The only time he left was when he was relocating someone and that was all business. He didn't get a lot of time away.

She rubbed her cheek over his before closing her eyes.

Trent took a deep breath.

He pulled in her scent. It had been so long since he'd just been able to quietly enjoy holding someone. Trent didn't allow himself this intimacy with his one-night stands. In fact, he hadn't done it with anyone since Melissa.

She fell asleep against his chest.

Trent turned the volume down on the television, so the sound wouldn't wake her up. Looking around the room, he noticed for the first time that she hadn't unpacked yet. There were still boxes stacked up on one side of the room. Also, she had several of her pictures leaning against walls where he guessed she was planning to hang them. Currently, the walls were bare.

Even in the dim light, he could make out the large pictures and he only recognized one. The others were new.

In Los Angeles, she'd had modern art and expensive furniture decorating her condo. Here, though, he saw that she wasn't using any of her old things. Except for that one photo.

Of a waterfall.

From one of their hiking trips when they'd first started dating.

Trent had taken that picture with her camera. They both had a copy of it, although his was tucked away in a storage unit.

Even if her tastes had changed in the years they'd been apart, there was still a moment holding them together.

The trip had been early in their relationship, but it was in that spot he'd first confessed his feelings for her. They'd made love in the water before camping next to the waterfall for the night.

He peered down at Melissa as she slept on him.

Trent believed she'd had no idea he was living in Brookside before she'd come. He was good at reading people. So were Magnus and Mac. Melissa's shock had been genuine.

Trent wondered about fate sometimes.

He'd run for months before finding a home in Brookside. Then, as soon as he'd grown comfortable with his life, Melissa had shown up, their destinies entwining once again. If he told Annabelle about his sudden interest in fate and what was meant to be, she'd probably declare Melissa his soul mate. She was a bit of a romantic.

Trent, however, was more of a pessimist. Or at least he always had been.

Until he'd found himself at Melissa's house with her in his arms.

What in the hell am I doing?

This had to be one of the biggest mistakes of his life. Melissa didn't need to get mixed up with him again. He also didn't know if he could trust her again. She'd turned her back on him once. That had nearly destroyed him. If the same thing happened again, he wouldn't survive it.

In his pocket, his cell buzzed.

It took some maneuvering before he was able to pull it out without disturbing Melissa.

"Hello?" he whispered.

"Everything okay?" Mac asked.

"Fine," Trent answered.

"How's Melissa doing?"

"She's asleep right now. Took some pain pills, apparently, before I got here. But I think she'll be fine." Trent would make sure of it.

"Magnus is having the deputies drive patrol around town," Mac said. "Calvin and Duffy are in shifted form, running through town and the edge of the state park."

"Any sightings?"

"No, and after the excitement at the Graingers' place today, we don't really expect anything tonight."

"It would be stupid. They have to know we're on alert."

"Or they could be planning something big and don't care," Trent stated.

"They've been careful up to this point. I think taking a shot at Melissa presented a target they couldn't resist."

Trent growled.

"Calm down," Mac told him. "It's just what I think."

"It's a stupid move with her being a deputy."

"Well, we know Ranger Garth Stevenson is involved for sure. He'd seen Melissa at the sheriff's office and then the day before with Annabelle by the creek. He knew who she was and probably guessed why she was at the Graingers'."

"When I get my hands on him…"

"You'll have to stand in line behind Magnus and Logan," Mac said. "Right now, you need to look after Melissa. She's vulnerable in that house. And she doesn't know the town well."

"No one is going to get close to her again," Trent swore.

"All right," Mac said. He was quiet for a few moments. "And you're doing okay?"

Of course, Mac would ask. And he'd know if Trent was lying. "I think so."

"It can't be easy," Mac said. "Your history with her is filled with pain."

"Did you read the file I gave you?" Trent asked. He'd passed on the information about Melissa to Mac. Mac knew about their past and he'd needed someone else's opinion.

"I did. I spoke to Magnus more as well and what she did in LA was one of the reasons he hired her here. But

I'm not talking about what she did while with the LAPD. I'm talking about what happened with you."

"I know," Trent said. "But what choice do I have?"

"You could let one of us watch over her. None of us would let anything happen to her. Annabelle is itching to go over and take care of her."

"No," he snapped. "I'll do it." Trent might not be one hundred percent certain he could handle being around Melissa, but he also couldn't let anyone else watch over her.

Mac sighed. "Let me know if you need anything, okay?"

"Sure."

Melissa wiggled in her sleep then whimpered.

"I have to go."

"All right," Mac said. "Keep an eye out and call if you see anything."

"Will do," Trent agreed. He disconnected the call and placed his phone on the side table. That way he could grab it if someone else called. Which they would.

With Melissa settled back down, he decided to get her to a more comfortable place to rest.

He stood with her in his arms before walking down the hall. He followed Melissa's scent to her room, finding it easily. The bed was made with a black comforter and he pulled it back before laying her on the mattress. She rolled onto her good side and he tucked the comforter around her. As tempted as he was to crawl into bed with her, Trent wanted a better look at Melissa's doors and security.

He closed the door behind him and ambled into the kitchen. He got a pot of coffee started before walking to the back door. Melissa had locked it, but the deadbolt wouldn't hold against a good kick. She also needed a chain on it. Another lock wouldn't hurt, either.

As the coffee brewed, he strolled to the front door. Neither of them had locked it after he'd entered, which was stupid. He turned the lock on the knob, then the deadbolt. That was better, but she needed a chain there, as well. Next, he went to the living room window and noticed one of the locks was broken and wouldn't clamp down. He shook his head. Melissa was a cop — she should know about taking her safety more seriously.

He went over to his phone and sent Carter a text message of things to gather for him. Trent would take care of the locks himself. He strolled over and looked through the pictures lining the walls. He'd hang them, but the banging might wake her up. So, instead, he started going through the boxes still needing to be unpacked.

The box on top held some old high school stuff as well as her diploma and more from her rookie year with the LAPD. Trent picked up the box and walked it to what appeared to be set up as her office.

He stopped to make a cup of coffee before carrying it into the living room. He picked up the next box to sort through it. Towels and sheets. He took those to the linen closet in the hallway located next to the bathroom.

Trent felt good about being able to do something nice for Melissa. Especially since she was injured and wouldn't be able to do much for a few days. He emptied two more boxes, breaking them down and setting them by the back door, then refilled his mug.

It had been a little over an hour, so he checked on Melissa as he passed by the room.

She hadn't moved, so Trent backed out slowly.

He returned to the living room and went to the next stack. The first box had papers and files inside. He went to put the lid back on, deciding to put it in the office until he spotted a picture of Adam.

Trent froze, staring down at the photo.

His fingers were shaking as he reached inside the box and pulled out the old picture. It was a formal headshot of Adam in his uniform. He hadn't kept any mementos like this. Instead of putting the lid back on, he carried the box to the couch and sat down.

"Oh, God," he murmured. The next picture was of him and Adam standing in front of their police cruiser. It had been before they'd transferred to the gang unit. Adam hadn't married yet and no one had known that Trent was a shifter. Back then, he'd had tons of friends on the force. Both he and Adam had been popular.

It hurt to stare at the image of him and Adam when they'd been carefree and still believed they'd make a difference in the world. They'd been so young and innocent.

Trent dug out more pictures and letters from the box, looking through them before he found a file with the LAPD logo on it. Curious, he opened it. Fuck, it was a copy of the report of Adam's death. But there was even more. Melissa had updated the file as she'd worked through bringing down the bigots inside the LAPD.

The two detectives who had been in charge of investigating Adam's death had been relieved of duty not long after Melissa had begun to cause trouble. He smiled.

He peeked back into the box and saw a typed note.

Trent picked it up and had to read it twice.

Break it off with the shifter or you'll end up like his partner

He was growling while clutching at the letter. He gasped when he saw there were two more inside the box.

You're next and *Break up with the shifter or suffer the consequences*

Melissa had been threatened and never told him. Bile rose and Trent had to force himself to take deep breaths to hold back the vomit.

She'd never said a word, and Trent hadn't considered what she'd gone through when he'd made the decision to go public.

The more he learned about Melissa, the worse he felt. The information Carter had provided had been extensive. One of the reasons Trent had shown up was because of what he'd found out. That, and Melissa could have been killed.

She could have died in a field full of horses and she wouldn't have known Trent was still in love with her. He'd never stopped.

Taking the steps to forgive and forget was not easy.

Luckily, she'd been pretty drugged up, so he had time to get his head on straight. He needed every minute he could get to try to make up to her on the position he'd put her in.

Yes, Melissa might have turned her back on him, but Trent had walked away without fighting for her.

He'd proudly announced his shifter status without thinking how his actions would affect the people around him.

* * * *

Melissa stretched, crying out when the stitches in her arm pulled. She sat up in bed and looked around. The last thing she remembered was falling asleep against Trent. It had felt so natural and she'd been able to close her eyes and let go of the fear from earlier.

Now the ache was back in her arm, but she wouldn't take any more pain pills. She didn't want to stay loopy. She sat up in bed, glancing at the clock on the nightstand. It was a little bit before midnight. Had Trent gone home? She wouldn't blame him if he had. She'd conked out on him, after all. Melissa eased her arm from the sling and set it aside. The flesh wound hadn't been too bad. She'd had a deep gash in her arm but had only received stitches. Oh, it still hurt, but she'd live, which she was thankful for.

She climbed out of bed then used the bathroom.

After she'd cleaned up a little bit, Melissa exited for the kitchen, spotting the boxes next to the door. Melissa laughed, unsurprised the unpacked boxes had driven Trent crazy. He'd always believed everything had a place, and couldn't stand clutter. Which meant he was probably still there.

It shouldn't have made her so happy that Trent had hung around. He'd made it clear he had no feelings left for her. *But I can still hope, can't I?*

She'd been so frightened when she'd thought she'd been shot. At that moment, all she'd wanted was to see Trent. At least she'd gotten one wish.

If only she could figure out how to keep Trent around.

Melissa couldn't play the damsel in distress.

Trent wouldn't fall for her not being able to take care of herself and Melissa wouldn't be able to pull it off, anyway. Plus, she wanted to know if Trent had heard anything new about what had happened with her earlier. Maybe someone had even been found and arrested.

She strolled toward the living room. She could hear movement as she walked closer. Melissa stepped into the room and froze. Trent had found the box from when she'd packed up her office when leaving the LAPD.

The photo she had of Adam was in Trent's hand.

"Trent!" Melissa rushed forward.

He started before looking over his shoulder at her.

"I'm sorry." She tried to take the picture from him, but he moved his hand away. "You shouldn't have had to find that."

"He was so young," Trent said, his voice strained and quiet.

"Yes." She dropped to her knees beside the couch. Damn it, she didn't want Trent to hurt anymore. It had been careless of her to leave that box in the open. *But, shit!* She had no idea he'd ever even step foot into her house.

"I can't remember what we were laughing about when we stepped inside the store to get coffee. Adam stopped and I ran into the back of him."

"I know," she whispered. Melissa had seen the surveillance tape from the robbery. It had been part of the evidence she'd collected.

"I used to dream about that night every time I closed my eyes," he said. "But why can't I remember what we were laughing about?"

"It doesn't matter," she said. "As long as you remember him."

He turned to look at her. His eyes were red-rimmed and it was obvious he'd cried that night. Melissa felt horrible she'd brought back such hurtful memories.

"Hey." She laid her hand on his knee. "Let me put these things away." Melissa started to gather up the papers and files.

"No." Trent wrapped his fingers around her wrist to stop her. He tugged her closer.

"What?" Melissa was shaking with the possibilities of what his look meant. "Trent?"

He slipped his free hand at her waist, urging her forward. Melissa shuffled forward until she was pressing up against his leg. At the same time, Trent lowered his head. She was afraid of doing something to mess this up.

"I'm sorry," he murmured with his lips inches from hers.

"Sorry?" she repeated. It didn't matter what her question was, though, when Trent lowered his mouth to hers.

At the first spark, the first touch, the first taste, she surged up, deepening the kiss. Trent groaned as he nipped at her bottom lip until she gasped. He thrust his tongue inside and she sucked on it.

Oh, God, she'd never forgotten how passionate Trent had always been, but somehow, she'd pushed away how unbelievably good he felt. Melissa gripped his waist so she could hold on to him. If this was some kind of fluke or if it didn't last, she was going to enjoy every single second.

When breathing became necessary, he broke the kiss, but Trent didn't stop. He nuzzled his cheek against hers then nibbled his way down her chin to her neck. She tilted her head, giving Trent all the access he could want. He didn't disappoint. Trent locked his lips on the pulse point of her neck.

Melissa moaned while clutching at him.

Damn, oh, so good.

She ran her hand up his back, pushing his T-shirt away so she could feel his skin. Melissa wished that she could hold him tight, but being able to only use one hand made that difficult.

Trent pulled back then yanked the garment over his head.

"Please let me see you again," he requested.

"Okay." She attempted to remove her shirt, but Trent pushed her hand away.

"Let me help you," he ordered.

Melissa remained passive as, with a gentle touch, Trent removed her top. He was so careful with her injury that tears started to form in her eyes.

"Are you hurting?" he asked then kissed away the tear that had fallen.

"No," she told him.

"We don't have to do anything you don't want."

"I want. Please don't stop."

"Come here," he said. Trent helped her rise then pulled her to straddle his lap.

His erection dug into her as he rested her weight on him. Melissa peered down at him, but he was looking at the bandage wrapped around her biceps.

"It's just a small wound," she reminded him.

"I hate you were hurt. I should have been there."

That didn't make sense, though. Trent didn't work for the sheriff's department and she'd been following up on a case. "There's nothing you could have done."

"I wouldn't have ever left you alone."

"Trent." She tugged on his hair so he was looking in her eyes. "I..."

"I'm sorry I wasn't there," he said. "I'm sorry for so much."

"You don't have anything to be sorry for," she assured him. "It was all m—"

"No." He gripped her hips and pulled her forward. "Don't... I shouldn't have left like I did. I should have helped you."

Melissa was so confused.

"I want to kiss you until these past years melt away," he said.

"Do it," she urged. Melissa wanted nothing more than to forget about the past and enjoy Trent being there with her at that moment.

Trent kissed her again. Melissa allowed herself to lean into his strong body. They moved their lips against each other until she opened for him. Trent pushed his tongue into her mouth and Melissa responded in kind.

Her body heated. She needed to be closer to him. Melissa pressed forward while lifting her arms to wrap around his neck.

She cried out as pain flared from her injury.

"Shit, baby!" He cupped her elbow and brought her injured arm back down. "If you hurt yourself, we're going to have to stop."

"No!" she begged. Melissa felt as if every fantasy she'd dreamed up in the past five years was coming true.

"Then let me do the work," he demanded. He rose and she had to wrap her good arm around his shoulder to keep from falling. Not that he'd have let her. Trent placed his palm on her ass as he carried her out of the living room to her bed.

Trent laid her softly on the bed before taking a step back to look at her.

Melissa bit her lip. "What?" she asked.

"You're beautiful."

She laughed. "Thank you?"

"We're going to talk. We have a lot of things we need to work out."

Melissa nodded. "I know."

"But first, I want to make love to you," he said. "I want to smell myself on you again. Just like I used to."

"Yes," she pleaded.

"Don't move too much and hurt yourself."

Melissa shook her head. She'd do her best, but she couldn't make him a promise like that.

He grinned, a deliciously wicked look she never imagined would be hers again.

"Hurry," she ordered.

Trent leaned down and slowly peeled the clothes from her body. Melissa kept her gaze on him the entire time he undressed her. She wanted to see every small detail of him while he watched in return. Trent's gaze practically glowed as he peered down.

When she was naked, he trailed his fingers from her collarbone down her body to her toe.

Melissa shuddered and wiggled around.

Trent growled. The animalistic sound echoed in the quiet room. It should have scared her. They hadn't been together long when she'd learned he was a shifter. After Trent had left, she'd started to think of ways he'd been different from everyone else. But she'd never feared him. Not when she'd broken his heart and not now when he looked ready to pounce on her.

"Show me who you really are," she told him. They'd never had this chance and now Melissa was going to let Trent be who he truly was.

He nodded then quickly disrobed. He didn't take the same care with his clothes as he did hers. He'd undressed her, even taking time to fold up her garments, but he stripped so fast he dropped his own garments to the carpet.

"Jeez," she breathed. He was fucking hot. With his muscles bulging, his cock leaking and him staring at her, Melissa could just look at him all night.

Trent palmed his cock then stroked himself.

She lifted to sit up and licked her lips. She wanted to taste him. It had been so long. "Come here," she begged.

He closed the distance. Melissa reached for him and covered his hand with hers. His shaft jumped when she touched him. Trent dropped his head back and groaned as she jacked him. He moved his hips in small thrusts, sliding his cock through her hold.

"I've missed your touch," he murmured.

"I missed touching you," she responded. Melissa leaned farther across the mattress so she had her mouth inches from him.

"Please," he told her.

She peered up at him while moving the last few inches to take the tip of his shaft into her mouth. Melissa sucked on the mushroom head before sliding her tongue under the tip.

Trent bucked, pushing his cock farther down her throat.

With her hand on the base of his shaft, she managed to keep from choking.

"Sorry. Sorry." Trent mumbled.

No response was needed. Melissa continued to look up at him as she sucked him deeper.

Trent gripped her head gently before tangling his fingers in her hair. He kept the pressure on her as she moved up and down on his cock, bringing him pleasure. It was a little awkward only having one arm to use and keep her balance at the same time.

He was breathing hard when he pulled out of her mouth.

Melissa reached for him, but he caught her hand before urging her to lie back. Trent followed her onto the bed, settling between her legs.

She spread her thighs as he slipped a finger through her folds to tease at the entrance of her pussy. Melissa was more than ready for Trent to take her. She hooked her foot behind his leg and pulled.

Trent chuckled, deep and wicked. "Trying to tell me something?" He plunged his finger deep inside.

"Yes!" She bowed her back. Melissa was indeed trying to tell him something.

Continuing to thrust his finger, he smiled. "You like that?"

"Not enough," she complained. Melissa lifted her hips in need.

He added a second finger before lowering his body down on hers. His shoulders covered her legs, trapping her to the mattress.

Melissa wiggled.

Trent went on plunging his fingers in and out. He used his tongue, bringing her pleasure. First, he licked at her pussy then closed his lips over her clit. She dropped her hands to his shoulders, ignoring the pain of her injury, and scratched his flesh.

He hissed but lifted his head and smiled.

"I want to feel you," she told him.

"Okay." Kneeling, he moved over her. He bent and kissed her.

Melissa pushed her breasts against his torso.

"You know now I'm a shifter," he said. "I don't need to use a condom. I will if that's what you prefer, but I really want to mark you in the most intimate way. I've never not used a condom. Even with other shifters. Can I have you that way?"

"Yes," she answered. Melissa was on a five-year birth control, so they didn't need to worry about pregnancy. Just the thought of having Trent's cum filling her had Melissa aching even more. She wanted that. *Marking.* He'd mark her as his. "Yes."

He nodded then gripped the base of his cock. Before pressing inside, he kissed her again.

Melissa closed her eyes, unable to look at him. This was what she'd been waiting for. To connect with Trent again.

"It's okay," he whispered. "I'm here with you."

She nodded.

He pushed slowly into her. Melissa held her breath. It'd been years since she'd been intimate with anyone. After Trent had left, she hadn't been making friends and hadn't even bothered trying to date.

"Fuck, baby," he muttered. Trent had his arms braced above her head and they were shaking.

He hadn't even entered her completely. Melissa lifted her upper body off the bed and attacked his neck with her mouth. She licked, nipped, sucked and basically marked him the only way she could while being human.

Trent thrust hard, filling her at last.

She cried out in pleasure. Trent paused with his eyes clenched shut.

"You okay?" she whispered.

"Fuck! I'm trying not to come. It feels so good to be inside you again."

"Perfect," she responded. "*Right.*"

"Yeah," he agreed. "Yeah." He withdrew then plunged back in.

The bed rocked under them, the frame knocking against the wall. Melissa didn't care. As long as Trent kept thrusting and claiming her, she didn't give a damn it the bed went through the sheetrock.

He held her legs up against her chest as he plunged deep.

It's amazing!

As Trent drove forward, Melissa broke apart. She screamed out while climaxing, giving her entire body over to him. She was his now. Whether Trent wanted her or not, Melissa wouldn't recover from this night. Even if he ended up walking away, she'd never find someone who could fulfil her the same way.

Melissa watched him until Trent thrust once more then froze. His muscles strained as heat filled her. *Yes!* Trent was marking her from the inside. *Yes!* He had her.

Chapter Seven

Trent lifted his head off the mattress and peered around the dark room. Melissa was lying across his chest with her injured arm curled by his side. He leaned down and kissed the top of her head. He had no idea what had woken him up, but now that he was, he needed to pee.

Trent slid out from under her, as carefully as he could. He glanced at the alarm clock on the nightstand. It was just after two in the morning. They'd cuddled as soon as they'd finished making love. And he had made love to her, even if he hadn't been gentle. He was still reeling from everything she'd tried to do at the LAPD. She'd even kept the case notes and files to follow up on the internal investigation on Adam's death. And she'd done all that after he'd left her behind to fend for herself. She'd proven to be stronger than him.

He climbed to his feet and strode across the room.

A quiet screech reached him.

Trent stopped and listened. Footsteps? He walked to the door, which he hadn't closed right away when he'd carried Melissa inside earlier.

Those were definitely footsteps. Trent glanced over his shoulder where Melissa was still asleep. Should he wake her? His gaze fell onto her injured arm and he had his answer. No, he'd take care of whoever thought they could break into her house. It had to be connected to her getting shot at earlier. Trent pressed his lips together to suppress a growl. He'd make whoever was stupid enough to break in, especially with him there, regret that decision.

If he wasn't a shifter, he wouldn't be able to hear the soft steps of someone in the living room. Or the rustle of papers. He slipped through the opening in the doorway. The lights were off in the hall, but there was light coming from the kitchen and living room. He didn't need it and unfortunately it would help whoever was inside with him.

Damn, his phone was on the coffee table where he'd been looking through the papers from the box earlier. He couldn't even call Mac for back-up. He had no idea where Melissa's cell was, either.

Trent pressed his back to the wall before moving toward the intruder.

A floorboard squeaked and Trent paused. The sound was getting closer to him. Changing his plan, he waited for the intruder to come to him. He didn't have a gun any longer. Not that he'd need it if the intruder was human. His weapons were part of his natural abilities.

Trent took a deep breath, counting the steps of the trespasser.

He saw the gun first, then the intruder's hand, before the stranger stepped into the hall.

Trent grabbed the wrist of the trespasser, grinding the bone with his stronghold.

The intruder cried out and the gun fell to the carpet.

Trent drew his fist back and punched the human in the head. He could smell that this man was human, but the mask over his face hid his identity. As the intruder attempted to fight back, Trent tried to tear the mask away. But the trespasser wasn't giving up. Trent took a couple blows to his ribs, making him stop going for the mask and defend himself instead.

Grappling with the intruder, Trent lost his footing and went down on one knee. He kicked the leg of the trespasser, knocking him into a table.

"Trent?"

Trent turned his head in the direction of the bedroom, where Melissa's call had come from.

At the same time there was a loud crash in the kitchen. It sounded like glass. Like part of the back door being broken through.

Fuck, this was not going the way he wanted. Melissa was injured and Trent had to protect her above all else. She was being targeted again and there had to be a reason for it.

Trent looked back at his opponent in time to see him raise a stun gun. Trent tried to roll out of the way, but the few moments of distraction had been enough for the intruder to recover and prepare. Trent cursed seconds before the stun gun was pressed against the back of his leg, the only place the intruder could reach.

His entire body seized up as electricity seemed to overpower every muscle he had. Trent had never been stunned before and as he lay on the carpet, staring up, unable to move his limbs, he hoped he never was again.

Trent could only watch in horror as Melissa stepped out of the bedroom naked and holding a gun. She aimed for the man Trent had been fighting when another shot rang out.

The sheetrock beside her head splintered.

Melissa ducked out of the way, retreating into the bedroom.

That was when the second intruder stepped into the hall. This guy also wore a mask and held a gun. He obviously wasn't afraid to use it, either. The second intruder was heavier than the first. Through the eye holes in the mask, he glared at Trent. Still, he was human.

Slowly, Trent was regaining control of his body.

"Kill him," the second intruder ordered. "I'll take care of the woman."

Grunting, sweating and desperate, Trent tried to get his arms or legs to work.

A loud boom and a shotgun blast pierced the night. The second intruder fell back, his weapon flying from his hand.

"Mark!" the first trespasser cried. He lunged forward, but Trent was able to lift his leg high enough that he tripped the guy.

Melissa came out of the bedroom with the shotgun still in her hand. Holy shit, she'd fired from the open doorway and saved them both. She stepped around the dead man and hurried to where Trent was lying. She'd about reached him when the first intruder had his hand back on his gun.

Trent grunted out a warning. Melissa turned her weapon on him, but the first intruder fired. The bullet missed her head by inches. The adrenaline along with the anger that filled Trent's entire being pushed away the effects of the stun gun. Trent kicked out his foot, connecting with the intruder's face. Blood squirted over Trent's face, but he followed up the blow with three quick punches. Melissa crawled over to him as the intruder's body fell.

"Are you okay?" she asked him.

Trent groaned. Fuck, he was either out of shape or those fucking stun guns were more powerful than he remembered.

Sirens sounded in the distance. *Back-up. Finally.*

"Help me up," he slurred. Trent was not going to be found lying on the floor when everyone else arrived.

"Are you sure?" she asked. "You look really pale."

"We're both naked," he pointed out. "We need to secure the one who's still alive and get dressed."

Melissa glanced over her shoulder before looking back at Trent. "I killed someone," she whispered.

Trent turned his head. It took all his strength, but he managed to lift his hand and laid it on her cheek. She covered his palm with her own. "He was going to kill you. And me."

"I know," she said. "I heard. I just never killed anyone before. I haven't even fired my weapon in the line of duty."

Most cops didn't. "It's going to be okay. They broke in here to kill you. If I hadn't heard them sliding the window open, it might have been too late."

"It was us or them," she agreed.

"Yes, now, help me up," he told her.

It took a lot of maneuvering. Once he was on his feet, Trent looked down at the guy who was still out.

"I'll watch him while you get dressed. Grab my pants, too, please." Trent limped over to the wall so it could hold him up. Melissa made sure he was steady before hurrying to the bedroom. She didn't look at the dead body. That was probably for the best. Even though Melissa had trained for this sort of situation, taking a life was never easy. It shouldn't be. Still, Trent had no qualms about what had transpired. Melissa had done the right thing.

God damn, his entire body ached. He bent over at the waist, hoping it would help him catch his breath.

"Trent!"

Mac's voice came from the direction of the kitchen.

"Mac," he yelled. Well, as much as he could with the whole gasping thing he had happening. "It's safe."

Melissa rushed out of the bedroom wearing a pair of plaid cotton sleep pants and a T-shirt. She held his jeans as well as the shotgun. She laid the weapon against the wall. Trent guessed she didn't feel safe quite yet. The sirens were closer to the front.

"You guys okay?" Mac asked as he stepped out of the kitchen. Glass crunched under his big boots.

"Here." Melissa bent to help him get dressed. Trent needed the assistance as he was still shaking.

"What's wrong?" Mac asked, stomping forward. He walked past the dead body but only gave it a quick glance.

"Stun gun," Trent managed.

"Fuck." Mac grabbed Trent's arm and steadied him before helping Melissa get his pants up his legs. Melissa buttoned his jeans.

He slid his arm around her back and tugged her against his body. It felt right to hold her. Now that the immediate danger was over, all he wanted to do was take her back into the bedroom and look over every inch of her body. "You okay?" he asked her.

"I think so."

Pounding on the front door had her jumping. Trent cursed under his breath. He was fucking tired and this was going to be a long morning.

"Why don't the two of you go into the kitchen? I'll let the sheriff in and take care of this," Mac suggested.

Trent nodded as the front door burst open.

"Sheriff's department!" Carl shouted.

Melissa sighed. "Great, never going to get my deposit back after this."

Mac grinned. "It adds character to the house."

Trent patted her back. While he was glad for Mac's presence, he knew, as the events of the evening caught up with the two of them, they needed to be alone. He didn't like to show anyone weakness and he expected Melissa would feel the same way. "Help me?" he asked Melissa.

"Yeah sure, sorry." She wrapped her arm around his waist.

"Calm down, Sheriff," Mac called as Magnus and Carl stomped through the front of the house with their weapons drawn.

"What the hell is going on?" Magnus demanded.

They'd just reached the kitchen doorway when Melissa stopped.

Trent nudged her forward. "Mac will take care of it," he told her.

"He's my boss," she said.

"I know, but let Mac take control. He knows what he's doing and will keep Magnus calm."

They shuffled forward.

"Keep Magnus calm?" she asked.

"One of his deputies was targeted for the second time in twenty-four hours. Magnus is going to be more than just a little pissed off," Trent said. "He can be a little overbearing when he's worried about his people."

"Oh."

Trent didn't know what she was feeling by her expression. She appeared confused. "Here, sit," she said. Melissa pulled out a chair for him and helped him down.

He groaned. It felt good to get off his feet.

"Jeez." She peered around and Trent followed her gaze. There was glass all over the tiled floor and the back door was hanging off its hinges.

"We'll get it cleaned up and fixed," he told her.

She'd moved away and he didn't have the energy to try to catch her. Melissa was biting her lip as she surveyed the damage.

"Get those fucking masks off. I want to see who tried to kill my deputy," Magnus yelled.

Melissa jumped again.

Trent growled. If Magnus didn't get himself under control, Trent was going to force himself up to confront the sheriff. Even if he wasn't at his best at the moment.

"Why don't you make some coffee?" he suggested. Melissa appeared to need something to do and maybe the task would help her settle.

"Coffee," she repeated. "Good idea." Melissa walked over to the counter and, even though her hands were shaking, started to fill the carafe with water. She worked quietly until the coffee began to brew. Immediately the scent filled the small kitchen and Trent started to feel calm, the familiar smell helping to ground him.

"Melissa." Magnus entered the kitchen with Mac and Carl behind him. "Are you okay? Trent?"

"We're okay," Trent assured him.

Magnus strolled over to Melissa. She had her back to them all. He placed his hand on her shoulder.

"Sure, fine," she managed.

Magnus turned her around to face him. From where he sat at the table, Trent had a perfect view of her.

"It's okay," Magnus said. "It's over."

Tears trickled down her cheeks. "I killed someone," she whispered. "He…that man…ordered the first guy to kill Trent and said he was coming for me." Melissa looked from Magnus to Mac to Carl then back to Trent. "I killed him."

"You saved us," Trent stated. He tried to stand, but Mac motioned for him to stay.

Magnus glanced between Melissa and Trent then straightened his shoulders, facing her again. "You did your job, Deputy," Magnus said. "I would have been pissed if you'd gotten killed."

"Me, too." Melissa wiped at her cheeks. She took a deep breath. "I think I need to sit down, though."

"Of course." Magnus led her over to the table.

Trent pulled out the chair next to him and brought it close for her to drop into it. He slung his arm over the back.

"I'm calling in reinforcements," Mac stated. He pulled out his cell phone.

"This is a crime scene," Magnus said.

Mac narrowed his eyes. "Yes, it is."

"This is officially the jurisdiction of the sheriff's department," Magnus told him.

"I'm not trying to step on your toes. But we don't know for sure that there are only these two men. My people can secure this house while you take in the suspect and the body," Mac told him.

Magnus huffed. "Fine." He pulled out his own phone. "I'm calling Logan and getting the Coalition here."

Trent stopped listening as the two men made plans and divided what needed to be done. He didn't care at this point. He turned toward Melissa. She remained sitting, but stared at her hands lying on the table top.

"Hey!" He grasped her chin, making her look at him. She blinked.

Trent pressed his thumbs against her neck and stroked. It was how his grandmother had calmed him when he was a kid. Trent had suffered terrible nightmares even as a child, but his grandma had come up with ways to comfort him.

Melissa made a quiet sound before leaning into his touch.

"Hey, Carl," Trent whispered. He knew the shifter would be able to hear him.

"Hey," Carl dropped down next to his chair. "Whatcha need?"

"I think she's going into shock. Can you get her a sweater and blanket or something?" Trent asked.

"Right away." Carl patted his shoulder before racing off.

"I'm cold," Melissa whimpered.

"I know, baby," he told her. Trent lifted her out of her chair and placed her on his lap. He'd share his body heat with her. Whatever she needed.

She buried her face into his chest.

Softly, he ran his fingers through the silky strands of her hair, much like he'd done when they'd been in bed together. *God, that was what? An hour or two ago?* He had no idea how long it'd been since he'd first heard the intruder slide open the window.

Trent wished they were back on the mattress under the blankets and the real world wasn't so damn fucked up.

Brookside was supposed to be a safe place.

This was where they brought people who needed to be hidden away before relocating them. How could some humans be responsible for turning everything he knew on its head? It wasn't fair.

"Here." Carl was back at his side. He handed Trent a large gray hoodie. "I got a blanket for her, too."

"Sit back," he urged Melissa. She straightened.

Trent helped her pull on the hoodie then wrapped the blanket around her shoulders. "Thanks," he told Carl.

"I'll pour the coffee. We'll get something warm into her."

Trent nodded.

"Trent! Melissa!" Annabelle shouted from the front of the house.

Melissa turned her head and peered up at him. "Uh-oh. I think we're in trouble."

Trent chuckled but nodded. "She's probably going to yell at us for a little while."

Melissa smiled. "At least we'll be able to hear it, since we're alive."

And there she was coming back. If she could start joking, she was going to be all right. He hadn't noticed she'd stopped trembling.

"There you are!" Annabelle cried as she ran into the room with Logan at her heels.

"Here we are," Trent agreed.

Annabelle dropped into the chair Melissa had just been in. She was grabbing for Melissa's hand and squeezing before he could warn her to be careful. "I can't believe someone broke into your house!"

"Yeah," Melissa said. "It hasn't been my best day."

Annabelle snorted. "Are you kidding me? If it was me, I'd be hiding out in my tree vowing never to come down. But you...you fought back. Saved both you and Trent."

"I didn't—"

Annabelle threw her arms around the both of them. "You saved my brother! Thank you, thank you."

Trent cleared his throat. "I did manage to get some punches in as well." *Okay, yes, Melissa does deserve the most credit, but come on, I took the first guy down.*

"Really?" Annabelle pulled back, although she did keep rubbing Melissa's back. "I heard that you got taken down by an itsy-bitsy stun gun."

He growled. "Those things fucking hurt!"

"I'm sure they do," she agreed. She fucking patted his cheek like he was a whiny child.

Trent glared, but Annabelle winked at him over Melissa's head. He huffed back. If it helped make Melissa feel better, he could deal with some teasing.

"I wouldn't have even heard them if it wasn't for Trent," Melissa said.

"So, what happened?" Annabelle asked.

"Hold off," Logan called over. "Wait until everyone gets in here so we can make an official report."

Annabelle waved her hand at Logan. "He's always so serious," she mumbled.

"This *is* serious," Logan responded.

"I know it's serious," Annabelle said. "That's why I made you bring me when you tried to leave me back at the bar."

"It's safer for you there," Logan told her.

"But I need to be here," she argued.

Logan was turning red in the face. From his expression, Trent guessed this was an ongoing fight. "You need to be home safe, where these lunatics can't get to you."

Annabelle rose. "If everyone is here, then it would be safer for me to be here!"

"Which is the only reason I allowed you to come!"

"Allowed?" Annabelle screeched.

"Uh, guys—" Carl tried to interrupt.

"I could have locked you in that underground basement of yours!" Logan threatened.

Oh, shit, this is getting out of hand. Melissa was stiff as she watched Logan and Annabelle argue.

"What?" Annabelle started around the table, but Melissa grabbed her wrist.

"Maybe we should all sit and drink some coffee. Everyone is really emotional right now."

Annabelle huffed.

Logan was already headed to her. "I'm sorry. I shouldn't have said that." He embraced Annabelle, pulling her up against his body. "It scares me these fucking guys are getting so brave. First, they shot at a deputy then broke into her house."

"I know." Annabelle sniffed at Logan's neck.

Melissa relaxed into Logan's lap again.

"Here." Carl set the steaming mugs of coffee in front of them. "Magnus and Mac are on the way back in here. They're getting Fredrick and Fabian started on hauling off the guy who's still alive."

"What about…the body?" Melissa asked.

"Already have the doctor on his way," Carl told her.

"Doctor?" she asked.

"We don't have a medical examiner here. We've never needed one," Carl explained. "I'll escort Doc

Phillips as he takes the body to the hospital. The Coalition is sending their ME to handle the case."

Melissa swallowed hard. "The Coalition?"

"It's going to be fine," Logan said. He and Annabelle joined them at the table. "We know you were defending yourself. You're a respected deputy in town. You won't get into any trouble."

She nodded.

"I was with you the whole time," Trent said.

"And what were you doing here?"

"Excuse me?" Trent glared at Magnus. "How is that any of your business?"

Magnus stared at him. "Everything part of a crime scene is my business. Now, start from the beginning and tell me what happened."

Trent wanted to growl at the sheriff, but Melissa squeezed the back of his neck. He shook off the urge to fight and nodded instead. "Sorry."

Magnus blew out a breath. "Me, too."

"As Melissa stated earlier, everyone is emotional. This is hitting close to home. And a lot has happened in a short amount of time," Mac said as he walked into the kitchen. "Duffy and Calvin are keeping an eye on the outside of the house. Carter is waiting for the identities of the two intruders as soon as we have them. Fabian is running their prints now."

Trent pressed his lips together. It helped knowing everyone was doing their jobs, but he wanted to get away from the others at the moment. He needed some time alone with Melissa. But he wouldn't get that until he got his statement over with.

"I called Brian Brooks from the hardware store. He's coming over to board up the doors, as well," Magnus said.

Shit, he hadn't even thought about that. "Thank you," Trent said.

"Trent, why don't you start?" Magnus suggested.

"Okay," he agreed. He tightened his arm around Melissa as she shifted to face the others at the table. There were six of them sitting around and one chair was available, but he wasn't letting her go. Not yet, anyway.

He cleared his throat. "I heard about what happened earlier and I came over to check on her. We had a quiet night, ate dinner, watched a movie then went to bed."

"Together?" Magnus asked.

"Yes," he snapped.

"Just trying to get a picture. If you were on the couch or something that is an important detail."

"Okay," Trent said. "I walked over here so my bike's not out front. I think the intruders expected her to be alone."

Magnus nodded. "Go on."

"I heard the sound of the living room window being opened. I'd already checked the doors and windows earlier and noticed how easy it would be to break in. I even called Carter and told him to order better locks," Trent said.

"You did?" Melissa asked.

"Security is part of my job. After you were shot earlier, I thought it would be best, so I called him while you were asleep," he explained.

"I thought you went to bed together?" Magnus asked.

"No, I mean earlier," Trent said. "After she ate and we watched a movie, she fell asleep. I carried her into her room. While she was asleep, I checked the security for the house before I unpacked some boxes for her."

"I knew that would drive you crazy," Annabelle said. She appeared pretty proud of herself.

Trent snorted. Okay, he might be a little obsessed with organization, but he wasn't that bad. "While I was going through one of the boxes, Melissa woke up and came into the living room. We…talked then went back to bed. Together."

"Talked," Annabelle teased.

Logan nudged her.

"What?" she asked. "We all know what they were *talking* about. I just said it."

Melissa laughed.

Trent appreciated Annabelle lightening up the atmosphere. He'd need it as he continued with his story. He winked at Annabelle and she smiled smugly at Logan. Logan rolled his eyes in response.

"Okay, so now you're in bed together," Magnus tried to get them back on track.

"So, we were asleep then I woke up. I wasn't sure what had woken me at first, but as I got up to go to the bathroom, I heard the window in the living room opening."

"How long between you going to bed and waking up?" Magnus questioned.

"Several hours," Trent replied.

"And you left the living room light on?"

"Yes."

Magnus was taking notes and writing something down.

"Why?"

"I don't think they were watching the house when you arrived. Did you come from the front or back?" Magnus asked.

"Front," Trent answered.

"So, they weren't keeping an eye out when you got here or when you were poking around at security. They would have seen you when you were messing with the window locks," Magnus suggested.

Trent shrugged. "Guess not. Does that help?"

"It's good to know. We'll try to get something out of the man who's still alive, but he might not talk. We couldn't get the hunter after Annabelle to. He lawyered up and refused to give us any other names."

"You think it's connected," Trent stated.

"I think everything that's happened in the past year plus the attack on Melissa is all connected. And I think I know who's going to be behind all of it," Magnus said.

"Garth Stevenson," Melissa said.

Magnus nodded. "Finish your statement please, Trent."

"After I heard the window, I crept out into the hall," Trent said.

"Without waking Melissa?" Annabelle asked. She scowled at him. "That's such a man thing to do."

Melissa was nodding.

"She'd just been shot!" he defended.

"Right." Annabelle leaned back and crossed her arms over her chest.

"Anyway," Trent said. Maybe he didn't appreciate Annabelle like he'd thought. "In the hallway, I heard the intruder and waited. He had a gun in his hand and I grabbed his wrist. We struggled and that's when Melissa came out. The second guy broke in the back door. The first intruder used a stun gun on me and when Melissa tried to come to my help, the second man took a shot at her."

"Bedroom doorframe," Melissa said. "The bullet should still be in the wood."

Magnus made another note.

"I was down, but the second guy ordered the first intruder—"

"Mark," Melissa said. "The first guy called the second Mark."

Trent had forgotten that. "Yeah, he did." He rubbed Melissa's back. "So, Mark ordered the first intruder to kill me and said he'd take care of Melissa."

"Did he say her name?" Mac asked. It was the first time he'd spoken since Trent had started his story. Trent hadn't noticed Mac's hands were clenched on the table. He'd been concerned with Magnus' reaction to Melissa being in danger, but Mac would be as angry as Magnus with Trent being involved. He'd have to talk to him later.

"No, he said the woman," Trent shared.

Mac glanced at Magnus. Magnus was writing in his notebook.

"What's that mean?" Melissa asked.

"Nothing yet," Mac answered. "It makes me wonder if this was a hired hit."

Melissa sucked in a breath.

"They weren't very professional," Trent pointed out.

"They were humans going after a human," Magnus put in. "If you hadn't been here, they might have walked right into the bedroom, killed Melissa and we wouldn't have known until they were long gone."

Trent growled as Melissa trembled.

"Magnus," Logan warned.

"She's not a civilian. She knows this," Magnus pointed out.

It didn't matter to Trent whether Melissa was a civilian or cop. She didn't need to hear about what could have happened.

"Sorry." Magnus lowered his head. "I wasn't thinking."

"It's okay," Melissa told him. "I'm not a civilian."

Trent opened his mouth to argue, but she turned her head to look at him. "Finish your statement. I want to get this over with. I'm tired."

And she was still injured. Scared. The adrenaline was, no doubt, wearing off as well.

"Melissa retreated into the bedroom while I was on the floor in the hallway. I was getting feeling back in my body and managed to keep the first intruder down. Melissa took Mark out with a shotgun. She rushed over to where I was struggling with the first guy, but I managed to knock him out. We could hear sirens by then and Mac got here right after."

"Okay," Magnus said. "A few follow-up questions before we get Melissa's statement down."

"Do we have to do this now?" Trent asked. "I'd like to take Melissa back to my room."

"It's better if we do," Magnus said. "You know that."

He did. As an ex-cop, he understood that the sooner after an incident they got the victim's statement down, the better chance of getting a real clue. But they had one of the suspects still alive.

"Let's do this," Melissa told him.

Fuck, she looked exhausted. "Okay." He had no choice but to agree. She was a deputy, and this was her boss. She wasn't going to shut him down. But as soon as he could get her away he was going to take her back to his room and make her sleep and relax. She'd already been through way too much in one day.

* * * *

Melissa held onto Trent's arm as she followed him through the back door of The Den. She was glad Magnus had offered them a ride. There'd been no way she could have made the short walk. Her legs felt like they weighed a ton. She was so tired.

"Almost there," Trent whispered.

He'd been so great. Since she'd answered the door and let him in, he'd taken control and made her feel safe. Even after the break-in and the attempt on her life, she wasn't afraid. Just exhausted. Melissa knew she could let go of the stress and Trent would be by her side. Sure, after she got some sleep, she had a lot of work ahead of her. Hell, she didn't even know if Magnus was going to keep her on the case. She'd been targeted twice in a twenty-four-hour period. But there had to be a reason for that. Why her? She needed to go back through all the research she'd collected.

"Turn off your brain," Trent told her. They were standing in front of an interior door. She didn't even remember walking down the hall to get there.

"Sorry."

"No." He turned and cupped her face. "You should be passed out by now. It's after five in the morning. You need sleep."

She needed him. Melissa nodded instead of correcting him, though.

"Let's get you settled." He unlocked the door then held it open for her.

His bedroom. Melissa didn't know what she expected, but she was disappointed to see it sparsely furnished. There was no personality in the small space. No pictures or decorations, or anything showing who Trent was now.

"It's kind of…"

Melissa turned. Trent was standing in the doorway with his hands in his pockets.

"It's not much," Trent said.

"It has a bed and you. That's all I need," she assured him. It was the truth. They could be in a cheap hotel in the middle of nowhere as long as she could lie down and be wrapped up in his arms.

"Good." He closed and locked the door before dropping her bag on a chair. "Do you want anything to eat or drink?"

"Bed. You."

Trent smiled. "Let's get you undressed."

He was gentle, but she still hissed when they tried to remove the hoodie she'd been wearing. Her arm was stinging.

"Okay," he murmured. "It's okay. Let me do the work."

Melissa allowed Trent to remove her clothes. He moved her with great care until she was naked. He kissed her quickly before pulling the comforter back on the bed.

"Climb in," he ordered.

She slid between the mattress and cover. He tucked the comforter over her shoulders.

"How about a pain pill?" he asked.

Melissa shook her head. "They make me stupid."

"It's going to be a hard couple of days. The Coalition is going to be here, and the investigation is merely getting started. Some good sleep would really be best."

"I don't want to be drowsy if something else happens," she told him. What if she'd slept through the attack? Trent might have been killed. She began to shake.

"Shh." He brushed the hair from her face. "This place has security cameras, a top-of-the-line alarm system and a bunch of shifters. You're not safer anywhere else."

Melissa sighed. She didn't like the pills. "I'd rather have you."

"What do you mean?"

Melissa sat up so she could lean closer to him. "Make love to me."

Trent closed his eyes. "I want to. I need to feel you're okay, but you're hurt."

"I need you," she said. "Please."

He stood. "Lie back. I'll take care of you."

Melissa returned to her back. Trent tugged his T-shirt over his head then kicked off his boots. He didn't waste any time removing his clothes. Just watching him reveal his body had Melissa hungry for his flesh, all of him, from his strong hands to his hard cock. Trent was unbelievably hot and for the time being, he was hers.

She didn't want to think about what would happen once things were over. If it was the danger keeping Trent by her side, she couldn't get used to having him around. Melissa might be tempted to drag out the investigation, but she wouldn't ever do that. Too many other people were in danger. Annabelle was still a target.

One of the reasons she'd agreed to return to the bar with Trent was because Logan was bringing Annabelle back, as well.

"Your attention isn't where it should be."

Melissa blinked up at Trent. He stood next to the bed stroking his erection. "Maybe if you came closer, I could show you what I'd rather be thinking about."

He grinned. "And what might that be?"

"If you taste the same." She licked her lips.

Trent shuffled his feet until he was leaning against the mattress next to her. Melissa leaned over to blow her breath across the head of his cock.

He groaned.

Melissa knocked Trent's hand away and replaced his fingers with her own. She stroked him before rubbing her thumb across the tip and collecting the pre-cum from his shaft. "Mmm," she said after tasting him.

"Please." He pumped his hips forward.

"You want me to take you in my mouth?" she teased. "Suck you down to the back of my throat?" Trent had always enjoyed her talking dirty to him.

He balled his fists. "You're playing with fire."

"Am I?" Melissa closed the distance to flick her tongue over the mushroom head of his erection.

Trent gasped as he pushed forward. Melissa closed her lips over his hard cock. She'd once known every ridge and vein of his shaft. She needed to take the time to re-familiarize herself with his cock.

She hollowed her cheeks as she pulled off before diving back to take him deep. With her hand wrapped around the base, she could control how deep she took him, even with him thrusting hard.

He'd begun to mumble as he gripped the back of her head. "Stop!" Trent pulled away.

"No," Melissa whined.

Trent pushed her back onto the mattress then flung the comforter off. He climbed between her legs while sitting on his knees. "I never forgot how beautiful you were." He ran his hand up her leg and around her hip then yanked her forward.

She wrapped her legs around his waist, Trent's cock at her pussy.

"Take me," she said. "Show me I'm still alive."

Trent growled. "Alive and mine."

She loved hearing those words. Even if they weren't true.

"Show me." Melissa needed him inside her.

"What if I want to play with you?" Trent trailed his fingers through her slick folds. He pressed down on her clit, making her arch and moan.

"Play later," she panted out. "Do whatever you want later. I need you now."

His grin was wicked, but at least he moved. Trent gripped her hips and lifted then moved until his knees were pressed against her lower back. He circled his hips, which brushed the head of his shaft against her.

Melissa whimpered. God, if she had the strength, she'd push him onto his back and climb on top to ride him until she was sated. She opened her eyes to plead with him.

"Better," he praised. "I want you to watch as I claim you. Everyone is going to smell my scent. I'll mark you from the inside out. Every inch will belong to me."

Melissa trembled, her desire strong. "Yes!"

He pushed in smoothly. She was so wet and ready.

"Put your hands over your head. Press against the wall and hold on," he ordered.

Melissa stretched out her arms until she could place her palms against the cool sheetrock. Trent held tight as he withdrew, then slammed back in. She cried out, pleasure swamping her. He repeated the move, rocking his hips and taking her as quickly as she'd urged with her demands.

Her hands began to sweat, the slickness making it hard to keep them flat on the wall. But with the way the bed was moving, she had to protect her head or be in danger of going through the sheetrock.

She cried out when her first orgasm was ripped out of her before she was ready. Trent never slowed down. He continued thrusting, only pausing when he needed to readjust his grip.

Melissa couldn't think, could only feel, as she climbed higher and higher in ecstasy.

He grunted, beyond words, using his body to communicate with her. She tingled from head to toe. She climaxed for a second time. As she dug her nails into his back, he howled out his release.

His cum filled her, warming her, claiming her.

Melissa wrapped her arms around his neck as he collapsed. She was too tired to move. There was no way she was going to have any trouble sleeping. He'd taken care of all the stress from earlier. She didn't need to think or remember. She could close her eyes and let Trent hold her.

Chapter Eight

Trent woke up with Melissa in his arms for the second time in twenty-four hours. He remained still, enjoying the weight of her body against his. Melissa rested her cheek on his shoulder with one leg thrown between his. For the first time in years, he settled.

He felt as though a boulder had been removed from on top of his chest. Trent could breathe. He was awake. Since the night he'd walked away from Melissa and his life back in LA, he'd been lost in a fog. It was hard to admit he'd been wrong and made some terrible mistakes. Trent had trained himself to stop caring about anything other than the people he considered family. Melissa showing up proved to Trent that he wasn't the man he'd thought he was. He was an even bigger asshole. He had a second chance, though. If Melissa could forgive him, they might be able to salvage what they'd once felt for each other.

Hell, Trent just hoped for a chance. He could be the man Melissa needed. He knew he could. Or at least he hoped. In the last five years, he'd changed. But so had she. Melissa was more open, and if she meant what she'd said, she was willing to work things out. Waking with her was the first step in getting her to agree to give him another chance. At least he was in his own bed and didn't have to worry about any more unexpected visitors. Here at the bar he'd ensure her safety. Even his hyena was settled, having her in his territory. She belonged with him. The animal inside knew it.

He peered down at the sleeping human. After he'd sated them both, he'd gotten Melissa comfortable on the bed to sleep in his embrace. He never wanted to move, unless it was a repeat of the activity they'd shared earlier that morning.

Damn, he'd never felt as good as when he was buried inside her.

He hadn't been lying. He'd claimed her.

Although there was a tingle of regret he tried to push aside. She'd been shot, almost killed for a second time, then he'd lost control and taken her too roughly. Oh, she hadn't complained, but a real mate would have put her needs before his own.

She moaned in her sleep before rubbing her cheek against his chest. Trent hummed with approval. That was a very shifter thing to do. She was human and didn't understand she was marking him with her scent, but Trent knew and that was enough. He ran his hand down her bare back, trying to comfort her. The clock on the bed side table showed it was after twelve. They'd have to get up soon, but he wanted to let her sleep for as long as possible. Melissa at least deserved that.

They'd agreed to call the sheriff as soon as they were up and moving around. The town was on high alert. All the shifters knew there was a threat to their kind and any humans were suspicious. Except for Melissa. Not that he was going to let Melissa out of his sight any time soon. She'd probably want to work on the investigation, but they had all the resources needed right there. *Guess it's time to let her in on the town secret. To show her what I do now.*

"You are thinking awfully hard for it being so early," she whispered against his chest.

He chuckled. "Depends on how you want to look at things. It's after twelve, so it's not too early."

She groaned. "It feels like we just went to sleep."

"You can rest some more." Trent didn't want her to leave his arms quite yet. "How are you feeling?"

She didn't answer for several long minutes. Not until she'd flexed, stretched and yawned. "Okay, arm's still sore. My body is pleasantly worn out, as well." Melissa grinned up at him. "Thank you for that."

He chuckled. "Welcome?"

Melissa rolled until she was on her stomach, gazing up at him. "I'm sorry you got drawn into my mess. I know you wanted to be left alone. Now, you've gotten involved in an investigation."

"It's okay," he told her. Trent meant it, too. When she'd first arrived, he'd been afraid he'd get his heart broken again. Now, the only thing he feared was not being able to protect her.

"No, it's not," she said. "I wanted to keep my promise. To not make you regret me being here. But how could you not? I killed someone last night."

"You saved both of us, remember?"

"Still." She shrugged. "You don't want to be a cop and I—"

Trent laughed. "Stop," he said. "I think I know where you're going with this and there is something you should know."

"What's that?"

"This isn't your normal kind of bar," he told her.

"I kind of figured that out." Melissa grinned at him. "Are you going to tell me what's really going on around here?"

He nodded. Trent needed Mac's permission, but he didn't think Mac was going to have a problem with Melissa joining the group. Hell, every other member of the sheriff's department helped out on occasion. "But first I need to tell you something that's more important." Trent was not going to chicken out. He would put himself on the line and pray Melissa felt the same way.

"Is it bad?" she asked. "Because I don't think I can handle much more bad news right now. I mean, if you think this is a mistake—" She waved her hand between them. "I guess I can understand that, but I don't think it is. I know I screwed up before, but I'm not the same person I once was. I've changed. I'll support you. I want to see you in your animal form. I won't—"

"Shh." He covered her lips with his fingers. "You're stealing my thunder here."

"What?" Her words were muffled behind his fingers.

"I know we can't forget the past. I don't actually want to because that would mean forgetting Adam, and that's wrong. But I'm the one who failed you. Not the other way around."

"I…"

"No," he said firmly. "I found the threats. You'd been dealing with more than I ever knew." Trent removed his hand. "I didn't think about what my coming out as a shifter would do to you."

"I should have told you," she said. "I thought I could handle it. Until Adam was killed, then I knew he wasn't the only one who was going to get hurt."

"I understand now. I shouldn't have put that on you," he said. "I'm in awe of everything you tried to do after I left."

"I wish I could have done more," she told him. Melissa pushed up onto her elbows. "I tried, I really did. The LAPD is a big organization."

"You made changes happen," he pointed out. "You mattered."

"So you forgive me?"

"There's nothing to forgive. Do you forgive me? For leaving you behind? Letting you deal with what should have been my mess?"

"I never blamed you for leaving," she said. "I would have probably have done the same thing. I didn't have as much to lose as you did."

He shook his head. Trent didn't think Melissa would have run, but it was too late to go back and change things. He could only hope that meant they had a future. "I'm glad you ended up here. I know now I would have spent the rest of my life being alone because you weren't by my side."

She stiffened. Trent couldn't look at her, though. It had to be easier to say the words if he didn't have to see her eyes.

"What are you saying, Trent?"

"Even though I don't deserve you, I can't let you go now I've had you again."

"I don't want you to," she said. Melissa tucked her knees under her then climbed up and straddled his waist. He placed his hands on her hips to hold her steady.

"I'm still in love with you," he confessed.

She gasped.

Finally, he raised his gaze to meet hers.

"I never stopped loving you," she told him.

He yanked her forward and took her lips in a passionate, almost desperate, kiss. Complete elation filled him. Not only did Melissa still have feelings for him, she was willing to forgive him. It didn't matter if it took the rest of his life, he was going to make up for his behavior.

Trent couldn't help the need to touch her. He ran his hands up and down her back as she leaned against him. Her breasts pressed against his chest while she wiggled around.

"I want you again," she whispered against his lips.

He cupped her ass. "I was rough last night. Your body is still healing." If there was a way he could change her into a shifter so she'd benefit from their special DNA, he would. Sadly, there wasn't a way to change humans into shifters. Only being born a shifter was possible.

"Please, Trent," she said. "I'm fine and I need you."

"I need you, too," he confessed. He might be a bastard, but he couldn't resist her.

She reached around to grasp his cock. He pushed up through her hand. "I'm going to ride you this time," she said.

He groaned. That sounded good to him. Trent nodded before laying his head back on the pillow. This was her show, and he was going to enjoy.

Melissa beamed at him before stroking his cock again. It was hard to keep from thrusting, but he managed.

She laughed before releasing him then arched her back, which pushed her chest out. Melissa cupped her full breasts while getting onto her knees. As she thumbed her nipples, Trent realized it was going to be a lot harder to allow Melissa to have her way and not touch. She raised an eyebrow, a clear challenge, and he was certain she knew he was struggling.

"You're teasing me?"

She nodded. "I finally have you right where I want you," she said. "So you're going to lie back and let me be in control."

Trent squeezed his eyes closed, calling on his control before he nodded. If she wanted to torture him, Trent would have to push her to give him what he wanted. He reopened his eyes and smiled. "I'm ready."

Melissa pressed her lips together, showing her suspicion before leaning down to kiss him. She used her tongue and teeth, nibbling and biting. He had to clench his fists to stop himself from grabbing at the back of her neck. Instead, he allowed himself to melt. Her arousal was sweet and made his cock grow even harder. He lifted her hips so his erection was brushing against her.

She broke the kiss then leaned back. "Something you want?"

"You know what I need," he responded.

"I do." She bent over him, this time placing her nipple next to his mouth.

Trent kissed then sucked on the hard nub, enjoying the way she clutched at his shoulders. She always loved his mouth. Once it was time for him to be in control, he'd worship her with his tongue for hours.

She gasped and pulled away to peer down at him. "You play dirty."

"I'll show you dirty." Fuck, he wanted to flip her onto her back and bury his cock deep.

Melissa laughed. "I hope you do." She reached back and grasped his shaft again. "But first, I'm going to use you like I've been dreaming about for years."

Trent clenched his teeth as Melissa positioned herself. She gazed at him while lowering down, taking his cock inside her tight pussy.

"Jesus Christ!" he shouted. Trent shook with the need to thrust up. She was torturing him with her slow pace.

Melissa dug her nails into his pecs. She threw her head back as she moaned in pleasure.

She was so beautiful. Trent watched her, refusing to take his gaze off her. She was like a goddess lost in the passion of their bodies coming together. Finally, she took him all the way in.

"Touch me," she whispered.

Thank God. Trent leaned up so he could kiss along her collarbone to her soft neck. As he used his lips, he also ran his palms over her ass and lifted her. Trent pulled out slightly before pushing back up.

Melissa sighed, the soft sound barely leaving her lips.

He repeated the action, allowing her to enjoy the rocking movement. He kept his pace slow, enjoying the way her inner muscles tried to keep his cock buried.

"More," she demanded. Melissa pushed on his chest until he was flat against the mattress again. She dug her knees into the bed and raised herself to ride him, hard and fast.

Trent's body tingled like he'd been electrocuted. He grunted as his slick palms slid against her hips. Melissa's pace sped up more. It wasn't going to take long for him to completely lose it.

"Yes!" she cried out.

"Yes," he repeated. Trent grabbed her thighs and began to plunge up. He met each stroke with an enthusiastic thrust.

They raced toward their own climaxes, urging each other on with words and sounds. The end was coming too fast. She bit at his shoulder just as she convulsed. Her pussy clamped down so hard he shouted as he continued to drive into her.

He held Melissa against his chest, chasing his own orgasm. He thrust, withdrew, striving to claim her.

Melissa turned her head, kissing him deeply.

Trent sucked on her tongue while he started to come. He filled her pussy. He knew even after she showered, she'd still smell like him.

The primal animal part of him wanted to howl.

He threw his head back and yelled as the final bursts of his seed claimed her. Trent let his hips fall back to the mattress and closed his eyes. He was tired again. But this time, it was a sated and happy, body exhausted and heart full, kind of tired.

"Wow," she whispered.

He chuckled. "We could stay here forever."

"We'll need to eat eventually."

Trent grunted. At the moment, he didn't care about anything but her. Melissa pulled up and his half-hard cock slipped from her body. Trent reached over and tugged her against his side.

She rested her head on his shoulder, just the way she'd lain when they'd woken up. He pressed a kiss to her forehead before he ran his fingers though her hair.

They needed to shower and get some food. Then find the others and call the sheriff. There was a full day ahead of them.

Someone pounded on his door.

Melissa started to laugh. "At least they waited until we finished."

He groaned. These were shifters and could hear pretty much through the whole building, even with them taking extra steps and putting in soundproofing.

The pounding came again.

"What do you want, Calvin?" Trent yelled. He could smell the panther though the door.

"You have about twenty minutes before the sheriff and his deputies will be here. They need to talk to you both," Calvin hollered.

Melissa stiffened. "Do you think something else happened?"

It had to have. After what he and Melissa had gone though that morning, the sheriff wouldn't bother them unless it was something important.

"We'll be out in a minute," Trent shouted. He turned to Melissa. "We should hurry."

"Something's wrong, isn't it?"

"I think so," Trent admitted. He rolled off the mattress before offering her his hand. "If we shower together, we'll save time."

She snorted. "Really?"

"Okay," Trent said. "I want to touch you again. This might be my last chance for a while."

She frowned. "I hate this. These people have no reason to attack us."

"Humans don't need a reason." He regretted the words as soon as he spoke.

Melissa jerked back.

"Shit!" He grabbed her hand. "I'm sorry, I didn't mean that."

She blew out a breath. "You did. But I can't really argue with you. I haven't seen the best of human nature lately."

He'd fucked up. "I have." Trent pulled her close. "You."

"Me?" She laughed.

"You came here to help people you don't even know," he said. "You've proven you'll stand for the shifters of this town. You showed me there are still humans out there who care."

"I'll always be human," she said, her words quiet. "Will the people in this town ever accept me? How about you? In five years, are you still going to be okay with the fact that I'm human?"

"I have to be," he told her. "I meant it when I said I was still in love with you. Whatever it takes, we'll work this out. I'm going to screw up." Trent chuckled. "Probably a lot, actually. But I trust you to call me on my bullshit."

Melissa grinned. "I can guarantee it."

"Good." He kissed her cheek. "Let's shower. We don't want Annabelle coming to get us. She'd probably try to climb in the shower with us."

* * * *

Melissa's stomach was in knots as Trent led her into what he called the family dining room. This back part of the bar was newer and homier than where she'd previously been. Melissa had been picturing a rough version of an old house. Instead the wood floors gleamed, the décor was modern and classy and the entire place felt secure.

This was Trent's home, so she should have known better. Still, she was surprised.

Trent held her hand as they stepped into the room where everyone else had already gathered. Even Magnus had arrived.

"Hey!" Annabelle was the first one to spot them. She jumped up and rushed over to Melissa's side. "How are you feeling?"

"I'm okay," Melissa was quick to assure her.

Annabelle narrowed her eyes. "Really?"

She nodded. "My arm's a little sore, but it isn't too bad." Melissa looked over at Trent. "Trent's been taking good care of me."

Annabelle beamed. "I knew as soon as he got his head out of his ass he'd do the right thing."

"Hey," Trent complained. He released Melissa so he could push Annabelle toward Logan. "What did I tell you about her needing a leash?"

Logan tried to smile, but it was obvious it took effort.

Trent must have noticed, as well. "So, what's going on?"

Mac gestured for them to sit at the table.

Trent ran his hand over her shoulder before placing his palm against her lower back, urging her forward. She sat next to Annabelle, leaving Trent to take the seat on her right.

Annabelle was pouring them cups of coffee as everyone else settled back down. "You need to eat," Annabelle said. She motioned to another woman to bring over plates.

Melissa wanted to protest. The knowledge that something was wrong took her appetite.

"Don't argue," Annabelle warned. "You're going to need your strength. We all are." She sounded upset. It was Logan who reached for her, though.

"What?" Trent barked.

"About an hour ago, I stopped by Deputy Garcia's house. I tried calling him and he'd not been answering. I decided to check on him. He was on call last night at the office, so he knew what was going on. I hoped he was merely sleeping after the long night shift," Magnus said. His hands shook as badly as his voice.

"He wasn't asleep," Trent guessed.

"It appears he was ambushed as he walked in his front door. I smelt four humans," Magnus said. "He never stood a chance."

Melissa swallowed hard and put her hand over her mouth.

She might have been new to the town, but she'd worked with James Garcia. He'd told her on her first day he liked working the night shift because nothing ever happened and he could sit at the station by himself and play solitaire on his computer. He'd been the oldest of them, including Magnus. He'd also been out of shape with a beer gut and receding hairline. He'd liked apples and sunflower seeds.

Tears filled her eyes.

He'd told old stupid jokes and never smiled. Melissa had really liked him.

Annabelle gasped out a sob before Logan pulled her against his chest.

Trent wrapped his arm around Melissa's shoulder as everyone else sat in silence.

"They killed a deputy," Mac said. "There is no turning back now. All their previous attempts had been unorganized and sloppy. But the attacks on Melissa and James were coordinated."

"I've issued a curfew for the town. No one is to be out after dark. I'd prefer if everyone stayed inside during the day, as well. If they can't leave town, they're to check in with us," Magnus announced.

"I have Fredrick downstairs working with Carter to track all our residents. I want to know everyone is safe," Mac added.

Melissa looked up. Mac watched her.

"I already decided to tell her," Trent said. "I just need your permission."

"You have it," Mac replied. "Get Melissa up to speed on what we can do here. I want to know everything there is to know about Garth Stevenson and anyone else who might be involved."

Logan cleared his throat. "I called in a favor."

Melissa peered over at him. He was stroking the back of Annabelle's head as she still had her face buried into his chest. Anger shone in his eyes, making them practically glow gold.

"There is a group of guys who owe me one," Logan said. "They were the first Coalition agents after we came out. These are some badass guys. They'll be here in a couple of hours."

"Coalition agents?" Trent asked.

"We need them," Logan said. "We don't have any idea how many people are behind this. Enough to attack you and Melissa while setting up to kill James. Right now, they're targeting law enforcement. Trying to get rid of anyone who can stop them. The bar will be next. They've already targeted this place before."

"What do you think they want?" There had to be a reason for Grant to attack the town.

"I believe they want to wipe out all the shifters here," Logan stated.

"But…" Melissa didn't know how to respond. It couldn't even be possible. "Someone would notice."

"Eventually," Magnus said. "Having Logan and the other Coalition agents here complicates their plan. Someone is going to notice if Logan, Fabian and Fredrick go missing. But without them, we're pretty much on our own. We don't have much contact with other people."

"Delivery drivers," Trent said. "We get supplies for all the stores up here."

Magnus shook his head. "You're right. It doesn't make sense to us, but this has to have been in the works for a long time. There are too many people involved for them not to have thought this through."

"Think about it," Annabelle said, lifting her head. "If they got rid of the shifters, they'd take over the town. Move in and carry on like nothing is wrong. The land is valuable, being so close to the state park. We've gotten offers for a decade, trying to buy up pieces of the town. We don't sell because we want to keep it for shifters."

"Christ," Trent exclaimed. "There's no telling who is really behind this. Grant could be working for someone else."

"What was the name of the developer who came around a couple of years ago?" Mac asked.

Melissa didn't know who they were talking about, but she could put the pieces together. If a developer wanted the land so much, he might have hired Grant to try to chase them away. Shooting at the shifters when they were out running would have the shifters feeling unsafe. But would they have moved on to murder if the first plan hadn't worked?

"Damn it." Trent pounded his fist on the table. "I can't remember the asshole's name."

"Me, neither," Mac admitted.

"I think I threw his card away," Magnus added.

"Carter will be able to find it," Annabelle said. "He did a complete background check as soon as that man arrived."

"That's right," Trent agreed.

"Okay," Mac said. "We need to set up a plan."

Magnus cleared his throat. "This is still a sheriff's department operation."

Mac grinned. It made the huge biker look years younger. Melissa didn't think Mac did a whole lot of smiling. "Of course, Sheriff."

Magnus rolled his eyes. "I mean it."

"So, tell us what you want to do," Trent responded.

"Have Carter find the file on the developer. In the meantime, the rest of us need to go out and help the residents. If they can leave, great, help them load up and get on the road. Anyone who stays needs to keep a phone with them. Have them report any suspicious activity or problems to Carter," Magnus said.

"What about the station?" Melissa asked. It was normal for them to transfer the phones to the deputy on call. But that still left the station vulnerable.

"Fabian and Carl took the prisoner to the Coalition office. They'll about be back in town. They don't know about James yet."

"Shit," Trent spat. "Carl is going to take this hard."

"So will everyone else in town," Magnus said. "I'm keeping it quiet, but eventually someone is going to figure it out. I had doc take his body to the hospital."

"Carter and Fredrick will monitor the residents and us. Trent and Melissa, go north and make sure all the residents know the plan and leave or stay inside. Logan and Annabelle, take the south. I sent Calvin and Duffy east already to check the entrance to town. That leaves the west for me," Mac said.

"And me," Magnus put in.

"You need to be seen around town," Mac told him. "Kelly will stay and keep the bar locked down here. With Carter and Fredrick downstairs, she'll be safe enough."

"We'll only have a few hours to get everything locked down tight," Trent said.

"Meet back here by four, no matter what," Magnus ordered. "Logan's friends should be here by then and we'll come up with a plan of attack. We're not going to play defense. When they come, we'll be ready."

"The zombie plan," Trent laughed. "Are you fucking kidding me?"

"What?" Melissa asked.

Annabelle giggled. "Carter got us all into playing an online zombie game. He made an exit plan for if the zombies ever came. It's quite brilliant."

"If we can survive the zombie apocalypse, then a couple of humans won't be that hard," Mac agreed. He glanced up at Melissa. "Sorry."

She waved off the apology. Melissa was going to have to get used to the way this group threw around the word *human*. She knew she was more than the label. Trent didn't see her as the enemy any longer and, deep down, the others didn't either. She might not have been able to transform into an animal, but she was one of them.

"I can't believe we're going to use Carter's zombie plan," Trent complained. "He's never going to let us live this down."

That drew a chuckle from the group.

"I have one question," Melissa spoke up.

"What?" Magnus leaned forward. He was listening to her and that made her feel appreciated.

"You're assuming they'll wait until dark to attack. What's to stop them from hitting us when we separate?"

"Nothing," Mac replied. "But, for some reason, that's what they're doing. They're human and using human logic. They don't realize some of us are better hunters at night."

Trent chuckled. "They haven't done their homework."

"Okay." Melissa shrugged. "So, they're going to attack us tonight."

"That's my guess," Mac said. "Although they might be watching us today to see what we're doing."

"How is this safe, then?" Annabelle questioned.

"Our first priority is taking care of this town," Mac said.

Melissa hadn't been giving the shifters enough credit. They did set out to take care of everyone. This might have been a small town, but it took a lot of work to ensure the safety of all the residents. Even now when they knew the attack was directed at them, they were still making sure that the townsfolk were okay first.

"Anything else?" Magnus asked.

No one said anything.

"Let's get started," Magnus ordered.

Trent stood, pulling Melissa to his side.

"I'll get with Carter before I leave," Magnus said. "Call me if anyone comes across trouble."

"You didn't eat," Annabelle complained.

Melissa looked down at her full plate. She wasn't hungry.

"I'll get her something on the drive," Trent said. "I promise."

Annabelle huffed then turned on her heel. "I'll at least make you coffees to go."

"Thank you," Melissa murmured.

Trent kissed the side of her head before he motioned toward Mac. "Let me talk to Mac for a second."

"Sure." Melissa shoved her hands into the pockets of her hoodie. Everyone had cleared out of the dining room pretty quickly. She wandered down the hall toward the open bar area.

It was crazy—the first time she'd walked into the place, her entire life had changed. She could still remember looking up and seeing Trent after five years. The lights were off in the main area, but there was enough sun coming through the windows that she could see clearly.

What if she hadn't seen the post of a job opening in Brookside? It had been such a fluke she'd responded to the opening and Magnus had wanted to hire a human. It would have made much more sense to just have shifters, but fate or something had brought her back to Trent.

She wasn't going to let anyone take her second chance away.

"Hey."

Melissa jumped as Trent slid his arm around her from behind. "You scared me."

"I'm sorry." He pressed his lips to the back of her neck. "What were you thinking so hard about?"

"How lucky we are. What if I hadn't seen Magnus' ad for a deputy? Or he hadn't hired me?" Melissa spoke quietly, almost afraid to voice her thoughts.

"I have to think that, some way or another, we would have found each other again," he said.

"What if we hadn't?"

"But we did. That's what we need to concentrate on."

Melissa whirled to face him before throwing her arms around his waist. He was right, of course. What could have happened wasn't as important as the fact he was right there in front of her.

Trent cupped her cheek then lowered his lips to hers.

She pushed up, closing the distance and pressing harder.

"I brought you—"

They broke apart and turned to Annabelle.

"Coffee." She held up two travel mugs. "Sorry."

"It's okay," Melissa assured her.

"We need to get on the road," Trent said. He took the cups from Annabelle. "We'll go out of the front."

"Everyone came in from the back," Annabelle told him. "You have your key?"

"Yep." He turned to Melissa. "Ready?"

"Yes," she replied. Melissa headed toward the front door. They'd parked in the lot when they'd gotten there so this would save them from having to walk around the building.

"Hold these." He handed the mugs to her.

"Sure."

Trent pulled out his keys and unlocked the door. He yanked it open and motioned her to go ahead of him.

Melissa stepped out and almost slipped. Trent caught her elbow, keeping her on her feet. "What?" She looked down. There was blood — she knew what it was even as she stared in horror.

"Fuck!" Trent wrenched her back. The cups went flying out of her hands as she was propelled inside the bar.

"What's wrong?" Annabelle ran to them.

"Stay there," he ordered. "No, go get the others."

Annabelle frowned before taking off down the hall.

"Trent?" Melissa managed. She still couldn't process what she'd seen.

"It's okay," he said. "Just stay in here." He was peeking around the edge of the door frame. Then he cursed quietly.

"What?" Melissa was afraid to ask.

"Son of a bitch," he muttered.

"Trent? You okay?" Mac ran in.

"Keep the girls inside," Trent ordered. "Where's Carter? Why was no one watching the fucking cameras?"

"What are you talking about?" Mac demanded.

"Someone left us a present right on our fucking doorstep." Trent whirled around. "And no one saw?"

Mac shouldered past Trent. There came a string of curses before he stomped back inside. He slammed the door behind him.

Logan, Magnus and Annabelle joined them.

"Trent, take Logan out of the back door and come around to the front. Make sure you watch where you're stepping," Mac ordered. He pulled out his phone. "Carter, come to the front. Bring the portable camera monitor."

"What is going on?" Annabelle cried.

"It was a deer," Melissa said, still in shock.

"Shh," Trent soothed. "It's okay."

Melissa shuddered. Someone had gutted a deer and dropped it by the front door. She'd been sleeping when some asshole had played a sick joke on them. Melissa's anger started to cover the shock. She looked over at Annabelle to see Logan whispering in her ear.

"Go with Annabelle," Trent told her. "I'll be right back."

Melissa watched him go. These creeps were even sicker than she had thought. She didn't know if this was a warning or what. Melissa straightened her shoulders. They wouldn't hurt anyone else.

Chapter Nine

Trent wiped his forehead with the back of his hand. He was exhausted, but at least the residents in town would be safe. He'd just finished helping old man Pritcher get his animals put in their stalls as Melissa finished talking to the neighbor. They'd been out all afternoon and this was the last stop. It was a good thing, too, since they were expected back at the bar soon.

He'd gotten a text from Logan that his friends had arrived.

Mac had also called a few times since Trent had left him to deal with the slaughtered deer they'd found.

Trent glanced back in Melissa's direction. She hadn't mentioned the animal since they'd left the bar. She'd remained vigilant throughout the day and Trent quite enjoyed seeing her in a law enforcement element. Melissa was quick and she knew how to talk to the residents. There was obvious distrust from the

Brookside folks, but Melissa never let that affect how she handled the situation.

"Thanks again, Trent," Mr. Pritcher said. The older man walked up and held out his hand.

"You know you can always call," Trent responded. Most of the town folk stayed out of old man Pritcher's way, but Trent liked the old goat. Literally—Pritcher was a goat shifter, one of a kind shifter. So very rare. "I really don't like you being out here on your own."

Pritcher chuckled as he patted the shotgun he carried. "I got Betty here with me. I'll be fine. As long as they don't go after my animals."

"You named your weapon Betty?" Trent asked.

"After my mama," Pritcher agreed. "She was the toughest woman I've ever met."

Trent laughed. "At least I know where you get it from. Seriously, though, call if anything happens."

"I will. And watch your back." Pritcher peered over to where Melissa was waiting by the vehicle. "And your girl. I hear they've already gone after her."

Trent raised his eyebrow.

"I hear things. Even way out here," Pritcher said.

"I bet. Keep your ear out for more than gossip on my girl. No one will touch her again," Trent stated.

"Good boy," Pritcher praised. He patted Trent's shoulder before he ambled off toward the house.

Trent gave one last long look around. The farm was as secure as he could make it. He had to trust Pritcher to take care of himself. He felt weighed down as he stalked toward Melissa and the vehicle. It was past time for them to be headed back.

"Everything all good here?" Melissa asked. She shoved her phone into her back pocket.

"Yep, ready to go?"

"Fabian emailed me. The developer who was here is no longer located at his old address. He closed his office."

Trent had been headed toward the driver side, but he stopped. "He closed his office?" That didn't make sense. The guy had been a sleaze and Trent had been happy to run him out of town. But there was no way the realtor was going to just give up. That was the reason Carter had collected a file on him in the first place.

"Disappeared, too," Melissa informed him. "Pretty suspicious, if you ask me."

"Very," he agreed. "Let's get back to the bar."

She opened the passenger door. "I'm kind of nervous to meet the Coalition agents."

Trent walked around the front of the truck and climbed inside before he responded. "You have nothing to worry about. I won't let them mess with you."

"If the residents here don't like me, I'm pretty sure the Coalition agents are going to be worse," she said.

He bit back a growl. "They will not say or do anything to hurt you." Trent trusted Logan to handle his friends, but if these agents even looked at Melissa cross-eyed, he'd take them down. They were federal agents and had to follow rules. Trent didn't, and when it came to Melissa, he'd play dirty.

As he started the truck, she sighed.

"What else is bothering you?" he asked.

"How do—"

"Come on," he said. "I know you. There's something on your mind."

She scoffed. "Are you kidding me? A fellow deputy was killed last night. There was a dead animal left in front of the place I slept last night. And we're using a plan that was designed for a zombie apocalypse."

Okay, fair point. "Well, when you say it that way…what's not wrong?"

She laughed. "Exactly. I'm pissed off."

That wasn't what he'd expected her to say. "About it all or something in particular?"

Melissa looked out of the window. "I think about it all. I talked to more people today than I have the entire time I lived in town. And, sure, most of them eyed me like I was coming to shoot their dog or something. Still, they respected my advice and just want to be left alone."

He grunted in agreement. As he drove down the old gravel road, they bounced around inside the interior of the truck. "The people here know what to do in case of an emergency. It's different to plan and execute. They're nervous. And you helped them today."

"I hope so." She reached over to lay her palm on his leg. "Is it wrong I hope they'll come after us and leave all these innocent people alone?"

"No," he told her. Trent covered her hand with his. "Because I want the same thing. I worry they'll know the surefire way to hurt us is by killing or hurting the residents."

"That's what I was afraid of."

Trent swung his arm onto the back of her seat. "Come here."

Melissa appeared confused for a moment, but undid her seatbelt then slid over. He held her close as she belted the middle seatbelt.

"Better," he told her. Trent didn't like her even being on the other side of the vehicle from him. If she was worried about the agents, it was up to him to make sure she felt as important as she was. "Now, I want you to listen to me."

She nodded before leaning her head on his shoulder.

"You are a part of this team," he told her. "Hell, you're actually one of the deputies supposed to be working this investigation. You are in charge here and don't let anyone push you around."

"It's hard when I know everyone else can rip my throat out with really sharp teeth."

This time he did growl. "Never going to happen," he declared. "Our friends know I've claimed you and I'll make damn certain the Coalition agents are aware of the fact as well."

It took a few minutes, but eventually she relaxed. "Is that why you wanted me to sit close? So, you could get your scent on me?"

Well, she wasn't stupid. In fact, she was pretty damn brilliant. He chuckled. "Part of it. More importantly, I wanted to be able to touch you."

"When this is all over, I plan to spend twenty-four hours straight of having you do nothing but touch me," she said.

"With my lips and tongue."

"Sounds good."

"It does," he agreed. Trent made the turn, taking them to the street leading to the bar.

"Keep an eye out," he advised. "If something is going to happen, it'll be between now and us getting back to the bar."

"No one reported seeing anyone strange around?" she asked. Melissa had lowered her voice even though no one would be able to hear them. Not with the rumble of the truck.

"Not that I've heard," Trent replied.

"Okay." She turned her head to look out of the passenger window.

Trent moved his attention to the area around them. Getting closer to the bar should have made him feel better. Instead, tension filled him. So much could go wrong at this moment. Beside him, Melissa had grown stiff.

His cell phone rang, which had both of them jumping.

"Shit!" Melissa slapped her hand across her heart.

"Fuck," he spat. Trent grabbed his cell from his jacket. Mac's name flashed across the screen. "Hello?"

"Where are you? What's wrong?" Mac demanded.

"Headed to you," Trent replied.

"And?"

Trent shook his head. "Damn it, the phone startled us. I have a bad feeling."

"How far out are you?" Mac asked.

Trent appreciated that Mac didn't question his feeling. "Ten minutes."

Mac shouted something before returning to Trent. "Calvin and Duffy are riding to you. They'll meet you halfway and escort you back."

"Great." Trent looked over at Melissa. "Thanks."

"Just get here safely," Mac ordered then hung up.

Melissa glanced over at him before returning to stare out of the window. "Everything okay?"

"Mac is sending us some company," Trent told her.

"All right."

The sun was still bright, but Trent knew it would be setting soon. It didn't give them much time to plan, although he expected the humans to attack later in the night or early morning like they had before.

He heard the bikes before he saw them. "Up ahead."

Melissa blew out a breath. "I don't know your team well, but they're a damn good sight."

"Yeah." That reminded him he hadn't told Melissa what went on at the bar. He slowed, allowing Calvin and Duffy to circle around to ride either side of their truck. "So the bar…"

"The one with a hacker capable of breaking into the LAPD and pulling up files?" she asked. "Yes, let's talk about that."

"Mac runs an underground network for shifters who need help," Trent blurted the information right out.

"An underground network?" she repeated.

"Before the shifter community became public, we would help relocate shifters who had drawn the attention of humans," Trent informed her.

"Makes sense. Actually, it makes a lot of sense. I never thought about how much you had to hide beforehand."

"We learned early and knew our survival depended on keeping our secrets. Still, sometimes a human would see someone transform or a shifter would tell the wrong person. Mac helped them start a new life."

"And now you're public?" she asked.

"We still relocate shifters. Not everyone is happy we're around and some target the shifters," he said.

"Just like here."

"Funnily enough, yes." Trent nodded. "We also take in domestic survivors. Mac has a history with that sort of situation, but it's his story to tell."

"I understand," Melissa said. She began to laugh.

"What?" he asked. Trent had to be missing something.

"You didn't give up law enforcement."

He scoffed. "I certainty did."

"Okay, yes, you stopped playing by the rules. Somehow, you still managed to land someplace that needed you. You're still helping people."

He shrugged. "In my own way, I guess."

"In the way that makes it possible for you to flip off the police and do what you've always wanted. To protect those who need it the most."

Trent hadn't thought about why he'd joined Mac's group that way, but she was right. He peered in one side mirror then the other to check on his friends. They were still driving right by his side. Just like the team they were.

"So, Magnus and the other deputies help?"

"When needed," he admitted. "We do try to keep them out of it as much as possible, but sometimes we need help."

"Logan?"

"He came to town in search of a woman who we'd helped," Trent said. "He fell in love with Annabelle and never left."

"He's in on it, too?"

"He knows about it, but we do keep him clean. He's a federal employee, after all."

"I want to help," she offered.

Of course, she did. "I'll let Mac know."

Trent felt as though he could finally breathe when he saw the front of The Den.

"Why The Den?" Melissa asked.

"Mac's a bear shifter. This is his den, where he protects his family."

She nodded. "More cars in the lot."

"Must be the Coalition," he guessed. "Mac closed the bar. All the residents know to stay inside by now."

"We're not inviting the park ranger in for a drink?" she asked. "That seems to be something you'd all do."

"Not during the apocalypse," he responded.

She rolled her eyes as Trent pulled into the parking lot. He ignored the parking spots and pulled right up to the door. He wasn't going to take any chances. The rangers probably didn't have a sniper with them, but Melissa had already been shot from a distance.

"Go right in," he told her. "Don't stop for any reason."

Calvin and Duffy turned off their bikes, Duffy in front of Trent's truck and Calvin at the rear.

"I don't see anyone," she said.

"We can't be too careful."

"You'll be right behind me?"

Trent undid his seatbelt then hers. "I promise."

She leaned over and kissed him.

Trent grasped the back of her neck, turning what was supposed to be a quick kiss into something much more. He wasn't just marking his territory. Trent was going to enjoy Melissa every chance he got.

When he pulled back, she had a dazed look.

"Now hurry in," he said.

"Don't break your promise." She slid over and put her hand on the handle. "I mean it, you'd better be right behind me."

Trent nodded. He watched as she pushed open the door before jumping down. As soon as her feet hit the ground, he was following behind her. Duffy had his back to the door as Calvin covered from behind. They made it inside the bar without trouble. He took a deep breath in relief.

Melissa spotted Annabelle first, which helped calm her down. They were inside the bar, so they should be fairly safe. There were enough shifters inside that Grant or whoever was working with him would have to be stupid to make a move on them.

Which made her worry more about the town.

It would make more sense to go after someone else.

"About time you got back," Annabelle griped as she rushed over.

Melissa had to admit it felt good to have a friend again. Someone who would worry about her if she didn't come back on time. Not that Trent wouldn't be concerned, but a woman needed a girlfriend sometimes. "We're fine."

"Come on, let me introduce you to Logan's friends." Annabelle tugged on her hand. Trent was following behind.

Sitting at one of the tables was a group of men. If Melissa didn't already know they were shifters, she'd still have been uneasy around them. These were some huge guys.

Logan sat at the table with them. Instead of beers, there were a couple of carafes of coffee and mugs scattered around the table.

One of the men, a dark-haired, scruffy-looking guy in biker leather, rose as they approached. He was grinning.

"Hello," he said. "You must be Deputy Bishop and Trent. Logan's told us a lot about you."

His hand dwarfed hers as they shook. "You can call me Melissa."

"Trent," Trent introduced himself next.

"I'm Jamie," the big guy said. "This here is Cody, Zak, Luca and Cole." He pointed out his fellow shifters.

Cody looked like a textbook Coalition agent, unlike Jamie, who could almost be Mac's biker twin. Zak nodded, but didn't stop scowling. Melissa took a step closer to Trent. Luca stood and shook their hands, giving them a warm smile, and Cole waved. She could she why Logan had requested help from his friends. Melissa would not want to go up against these five.

"Thanks for coming," Trent spoke formally. He placed his hand on Melissa's shoulder then pulled her back against his chest. The move did make her feel safe.

Jamie laughed before pointing at Luca. "You owe me ten bucks."

Luca groaned as Melissa glanced between the two of them. Zak smacked Jamie's back before he looked up at Trent and Melissa.

"They had a bet that within the first five minutes of us meeting someone, they'd show possessiveness over their female," Zak explained. "Logan did the same thing."

Logan shook his head. "Even knowing they're all mated, I couldn't help it."

"You're all mated?" Melissa asked.

Cody nodded. "Yes, we all have mates at home and are not interested in your women." He winked. "Even if they are very beautiful."

Both Logan and Trent growled.

"Too easy," Jamie taunted. He was practically bouncing around.

"Sit down," Zak ordered Jamie. "You're going to make them question our professionalism."

"Maybe they should," Jamie quipped. "I think all the time Cody's been spending in the office has screwed with his field training. I think he's getting fat."

"Fat?" Cody replied. "You realize I assign your cases, don't you?"

"Ohhh," Luca drawled. "Send him to Florida. He'll love it there."

Jamie lunged for Luca, but Zak stood and pushed him back into a chair. "Enough."

Trent snorted and Melissa agreed with his unspoken disbelief. These were the guys who were going to come in and save the day? They were a pretty ragtag group and were…joking? Cole hadn't said anything, but he was smirking. That was when she realized over the last five minutes the tension in the room had subsided and they'd relaxed. *Smart. Okay, so they might be able to help.*

She looked over her shoulder at Trent. He was watching the Coalition shifters, but even his anxiety seemed to have lessened.

"Have you eaten?" Annabelle asked. She'd been sitting on Logan's knee, but she moved to stand.

Melissa waved her down. "Actually, it seems every resident we helped today tried to feed us."

Annabelle laughed. "Yeah, they tend to do that. Kelly is making a platter of sandwiches for everyone. Carter and Fredrick are finishing up downstairs."

"Where's Mac?" Trent asked.

"He and Magnus are helping Duffy and Calvin board up some of the weak spots of the bar," Logan supplied. "Sit down and join us. We'll give everyone a couple more minutes then discuss the plan for tonight."

Trent pulled out the chair next to Logan and urged her down.

"So, Melissa, how did a human find herself in a town full of shifters?" Jamie asked. "That has to be an interesting story."

Trent snarled. "She might be human, but that doesn't mean—"

"Wait!" Jamie interrupted. "That isn't how I meant it. My mate is human."

"Mine, too," Luca added.

"Oh, shit." Trent dropped his head. "Uh, sorry. I…"

Jamie laughed. "It's all right, man. We all have to deal with prejudices."

"But we have one another's backs. It doesn't matter if we're shifters or humans or other," Zak stated.

"Other?" Melissa asked. *That's a weird thing to say.*

Zak side-eyed Luca. "Long story. Let's just say Luca over here has been playing with some unusual friends."

Luca grinned but he elbowed Zak. "Which I've been sworn to secrecy about. I knew I shouldn't have told you guys."

"Because we don't believe you," Jamie said.

Luca sighed. "I need new friends."

Logan waved his hand around. "I don't know if this group's much better. I'm still getting the stink eye about Annabelle."

"As long as you don't hurt her, we won't hurt you," Trent threatened, but he was smiling.

Annabelle groaned. "I just love all this testosterone."

"Hey!" Logan and Trent yelled.

"Trent, Melissa, glad you made it back safely," Mac called. He strolled into the main bar area carrying a platter of food. Magnus walked behind him with his hands full as well.

Trent stood. He relieved Mac of the food, helping distribute it around the table. Magnus passed out plates and utensils.

"I thought we could eat as we talked," Mac said.

"What about the others?" Trent asked.

"Calvin and Duffy are watching the front. Carl and Fabian are around the back," Magnus said. "We didn't want to risk the cameras getting hacked again. Carter is still pissed off about that."

When Trent clenched his fists, Melissa reached over and covered one of his hands with hers. Carter had been shocked after they'd realized someone had wirelessly connected to their security cameras and hacked them. Carter hadn't believed anyone had been able to get into his system, but someone had. There had been so much confusion and utter fury when Trent had ushered Melissa away from the irate man earlier.

Melissa really wasn't hungry, but she did pour herself a cup of coffee. As everyone settled around the table, she took the time to look over the two shifters who were mated to humans. Maybe it wasn't as unusual as Melissa had worried. Two out of five of the agents had chosen non-shifters.

"No one reported being observed or feeling watched. I find it hard to believe these people aren't watching what we're doing," Mac stated.

"It was quiet in town, too," Magnus reported. "Most of the businesses shut down so no one was on the streets."

"They might think they've scared us," Trent suggested.

"That's what I was thinking," Logan agreed. "They hit us hard last night. Going on the assumption the only thing they know about shifters is from television, we can't really say what they will do. Which worries me."

"How many do you think are involved?" Cody questioned.

"There were two who broke into Melissa's place," Trent said. "They've been taken out. That leaves the four we scented at James' house, plus any unknowns."

"What about the developer?" Melissa asked.

"Ramon Bustillos," Mac said. "He used to own and operate Green Mile Developing in Los Angeles. He closed his company down six months ago."

"Also at that time, he started to erase all his social media profiles. He's trying to make himself disappear," Magnus told them. "That, right there, makes me suspicious."

"He withdrew cash from all his bank accounts," Mac said. "He had over a million dollars when he disappeared."

"That's plenty of money to pay for help getting rid of a town full of shifters," Zak said.

"He'd make at least five times that amount after splitting up and selling off pieces of the land," Magnus said.

"God damn," Trent muttered. "This is ridiculous. They can't really believe they'd get away with this."

"Actually," Cody said, "he might have done it before." He motioned for Zak to hand over a file.

That didn't sound good. If this developer was hiring out the threats against the community, he was also using Grant's hatred of shifters. Maybe the developer hadn't wanted any of them killed and lost control of the situation.

Zak passed over the manila folder to Cody. Cody began to lay out sheets of paper. Melissa strained to try to see the file. Damn, she needed the enhanced sight that shifters had.

"Sweetwater, California," Jamie said. "Population was under two hundred people before Bustillos became interested in the land."

"Sweetwater also shared land with a state park," Cody told them. "So, that connection is what drew our attention."

"What happened there?" Melissa asked. She leaned forward, reading land titles that had been signed over to Green Mile Developing. Sweetwater was smaller than Brookside, but that didn't mean there weren't similarities. The link had been a good catch.

"As soon as Ramon started to show interest in the land, strange things started to happen," Cody answered. "There was an increase in crime, including arson. Eventually Ramon ended up owning everything he'd wanted. It took less than a year for him to replace the residents and start selling each plot of land."

"Was the town made up of shifters?" She looked over at Cody, since he seemed to be the lead agent.

"No," Cody said. "We can't actually find any shifters that had lived in the area."

"He got away with it once," Trent said. "Now, he's trying again."

"Instead of threats and arson, they decided to run everyone off by threatening the shifter part of the town," Melissa said. Which had been smart. The pieces were starting to come together. Except for one thing. "But Ranger Grant has some serious hate for shifters and Ramon was able to use that to his advantage."

"He does have a history of aggravation against shifters." Luca pulled out another file. He handed it to Melissa. She scooted over so Trent could see, as well. "He's a member of several anti-shifter groups on the internet. He also recently attended a big rally in Los Angeles with other humans who share similar beliefs."

"How in the hell did he get taken on with the park rangers?" Trent growled.

"We're looking into that, as well," Cody said. "We did uncover what we think is the reason behind Grant's hatred."

"Grant's brother Jesus was killed last year while hunting," Luca announced. "He was inside a state park, which we all know is illegal. He'd also targeted a shifter. The shifter defended himself and his mate by killing Jesus."

"The law is pretty clear we have that right," Trent said.

"There was a trial because Grant's family had some political backing. The shifter was found innocent," Luca said.

"Good," Trent said, pleased.

Jamie shook his head. "Four months ago, the shifter and his mate were killed in a home invasion."

"Fuck." Trent slammed his hand down.

"It has to be Grant." Melissa looked over at Logan. "Right?"

Logan nodded. "I think so."

Annabelle was biting her lip as she listened. She suddenly paled.

"Annabelle?" Melissa called.

"I know him." She pointed at the picture of Jesus Trent had passed to Logan.

"What? How?" Logan demanded.

"He was a regular here at the bar for a little while," she said. "He always ordered a crown and coke."

Melissa looked at the bar as though Jesus was going to be there now. Which was stupid, because he was dead. "Was he here before or after Ramon tried to buy the land?"

Annabelle squinted as she thought. "After."

"That's another tie to Grant and the town," Melissa said. "It's good you remembered him."

"Yeah, well, humans tend to stand out when they come here," Annabelle said. "I remember he'd told me he'd gotten turned around while hiking. That was how he found the bar. He came in over a few months. He seemed nice enough. He never gave me the impression he hated shifters."

"He might not have," Cody said. "From reading about the case, it appears Jesus went hunting quite a bit and didn't believe the government had the right to tell him where. It was a point of the prosecutor against the shifter who killed him that Jesus probably hadn't known he'd been shooting at shifters and not a natural animal."

"But Grant does hate shifters," Melissa stated.

"Yes," Cody agreed.

"And if Ramon somehow found out, he probably used it to lure Grant into the plan to get rid of everyone," Mac said.

"This is all good information, but it doesn't tell us how many people we're up against or what the plan is," Trent observed.

"No, but it goes to show Grant is the real threat," Melissa said. "He wants to kill and we need to be careful."

"I still don't think he'll come at us here," Trent said.

"I agree," Zak added.

"So what do we do?" Melissa asked.

"The only thing we can," Magnus replied. "We protect our town."

"How?" Annabelle questioned.

"We set a trap for them," Mac responded.

Melissa peered around the table. Even if they didn't know how many people they were up against, she'd rather be on this side of the line. Each person sitting around the table would protect the town and each other, with their lives, if necessary.

Chapter Ten

Trent walked with Melissa out of the back door. Carl nodded at them, signaling no one had been spotted around. He hurried to the forest line, bringing Melissa with him. Trent was more nervous about shifting in front of her for the first time than he would have thought.

He didn't like to transform into his hyena in front of anyone. Most shifters considered his animal form a lower class. The prejudice had stuck with him his entire life. It was one reason his parents hadn't socialized him with other shifters. Trent didn't want Melissa to look at him as if he was less of a man or shifter.

"Are you okay?" Melissa asked.

Trent stopped walking. He turned to where she stood, her back to a tree. She was so beautiful and he hoped he didn't fuck things up again, although there was a good chance he would. He'd just have to make sure during the good times, he showed Melissa how much he loved her.

"You've done a lot to help the shifter community," he said.

Melissa nodded. "I'm trying. I — "

"It's not going to get any easier," Trent interrupted. "The fight we're in isn't going anywhere any time soon. We still have so much more to accomplish. Until shifters have the same rights as humans, there's going to be a potential of danger."

"That's why I'm here. I accepted the position as deputy in Brookside because I've chosen my side. I want to stand with you."

He smiled. "I'm glad you said that."

"Is that really what's bothering you? The fact we're always going to be fighting against something?"

"No," he admitted. She was brilliant. "I'm part of a family here. Mac and the others accept me. We're a group of predators."

"Okay."

"My shifted animal isn't cool like a bear or a lion," Trent told her.

"You're a hyena," she responded. "I know."

"Hyenas are low on the power scale. Both in nature and in the shifter community," Trent stated. It was a fact of life and she needed to know. "By being with me, people, other shifter species especially, might look down on you."

Melissa smiled. "You think I care? I know who you are. I know what you can do," she said. "Yes, it's cool you can shift to any animal."

He laughed. "I'm glad you think so."

"Plus, I've done my research on hyenas. I have to agree with the main personality traits like being reliable, assertive and curious. I like when you get excitable, as well."

Okay, maybe she has done her research.

"I just want you to be aware of everything getting involved with me entails. This time I want to be completely honest at all times," he said.

She grabbed the front of his shirt before tugging him forward. "I'm very much aware of what being with you means. It means I'll always have a partner who will try to protect me while still allowing me to do my job. Someone who is going to love me no matter what we're up against."

"I will always love you," he declared. "And I can't promise I won't try to protect you, but I won't stand in your way. I know you need to do your job."

"And you need to do yours," she said. "So, kiss me and then let me finally see you in your shifter form. No more hiding."

No more hiding. That's what I've been doing. He'd pulled back from his old life before finding his home here. Melissa was drawing him out of the shadows and back into the sun.

Trent did kiss her as she'd demanded. How could he not? He pressed her into the bark of the tree while devouring her mouth. Melissa moaned, clinging to him. Even without meaning to, he found himself rubbing his hard cock against her as he tongue-fucked her mouth. He wanted to lay her down on the moist soil and claim her again, but they didn't have time. He drew back slowly.

Melissa slumped against the tree, panting. "Wow." She cleared her throat. "I'll stay here and think about how I'm going to ravish you later as you do your thing." She waved her hand around.

"You don't have to watch," he told her. Trent pulled off his T-shirt and dropped it onto the ground.

"I'm watching. I'm going to memorize every gorgeous line of your body. Even in your shifted form."

Trent wanted to demand she turn away as he transformed, but she had the right to see. Luckily, when he shifted, Trent didn't feel any pain. His body knew what to do once he was naked and kneeling. He pictured his hyena form in his mind.

The transformation was quick. His body stretching, fur replaced his skin. In just a few moments, he was sitting on his rump, looking up at Melissa.

She had her hand covering her mouth while she laughed.

Trent tilted his head, trying to figure out her reaction. He kept all human thinking and reasoning in his animal form, but sometimes instincts were hard to fight.

"That is so amazing," she said in awe. Melissa dropped to her knees in front of him. "I've never actually seen anyone shift before. I've only seen videos on the internet, but it's not the same as knowing the person."

He shuffled forward until he could put his head under her chin. He never thought he'd have been able to let her witness his transformation. The bond between them was growing. Trent was being accepted even after showing her what he'd always hidden.

She gasped then lifted her hands and petted him. Trent didn't like being touched as his hyena, but Melissa's hands on him just strengthened their connection.

This was the woman he wanted to mate with.

"Amazing!" she whispered.

He was glad she thought so.

"Coming up behind you!"

Trent growled and moved in front of Melissa. She rose before placing her palm against his shoulder.

"It's Jamie and Luca," Jamie called. The big guy strode into view with a smaller animal at his side.

"Is that Luca?" Melissa asked.

They'd discussed their shifter forms and it had been decided Jamie and Luca would team up with him and Melissa. Jamie would remain in human form unless the threat was too much for Trent and Luca to handle. It took a lot of energy for Jamie to change into his bear form. Plus Trent's hyena wouldn't see Luca's coyote as being as big a threat as some of the other shifted animals.

Logan's lion form would work well with Zak's tiger.

The many species involved in this operation were not new to either the Brookside people or the Coalition. Before coming to Brookside, Trent wouldn't have ever believed this was possible—working alongside so many shifters.

Luca trotted over to his side before lying down on his belly.

Trent wanted to move to place himself in front of Melissa again, but she was already reaching out to touch the coyote.

"Is it okay?" she asked Jamie.

Trent growled.

"I think it'd be fine with Luca, but I'm pretty sure Trent doesn't want you touching another man right now," Jamie responded.

"Oh." She pulled her hand back before laying it on the top of Trent's head. "Sorry."

"No problem," Jamie told her. "Your bond with Trent is still new. Anyone or anything that could possibly come between you is a threat. Especially as he is shifted.

Just be careful and make sure Trent can always see you."

Melissa nodded. "You better behave. No fighting with the good guys."

He sneezed, which was the best he could do as his hyena.

"Okay." Jamie clapped his hands together. "Let's get this party started."

Trent nudged the back of Melissa's leg then took off in a slow jog further into the trees. Their job was to search the state park for any scents of humans close by, or that had been in the area recently. It could mean hours of roaming the trails and off trail. But they would be able to track humans' scents to where they entered the town.

Magnus, Cody and Cole were circling the town to ensure the safety of the residents close to Main Street. The townsfolk who lived farther out were in a more dangerous situation, but the rest of the team was trying to cover as much ground as possible. That left only a few people to guard the bar, but most everyone agreed Grant and anyone else with him would go after easier targets. Trent wasn't so sure. The humans had already targeted two deputies. Trent would take out the biggest threats first. If the humans eliminated the sheriff and his department, plus the shifters at the bar, the residents wouldn't be able to hold out for long.

Melissa had appeared to agree with him, but both of them were going with the main plan. If he had a chance to circle back to the bar, though, he'd take it. He could feel it in his bones the bar would be hit sometime soon.

He led the way, with Melissa only a few steps behind. Luca trotted behind her with Jamie bringing up the rear. Trent returned his attention to the operation. At the moment, he was only picking up on nature and the hint of an upcoming rainfall. They needed the rain, but Trent hoped any bad weather would hold off until they'd rounded up Grant and his helpers, especially whoever was responsible for shooting at Melissa. Trent hadn't forgotten that one of the humans had taken a long-range shot at her. Like a coward.

There was a rustle in the bushes before a small rabbit hopped out. The little bunny blinked at Trent before scurrying away. Trent wanted to pounce, but made himself turn away instead. He didn't hunt natural prey.

"He didn't eat the rabbit," Melissa spoke behind him.

Jamie chuckled. "Raw animal is not very appetizing. We're still human, even with the change of form."

"So, no buying rabbits for him to chase," Melissa said. "Got it."

"Oh, I'm sure he'd enjoy chasing them, but he probably wouldn't eat them. But living this close to the state park is probably good enough for his hyena."

"You live in a city, though, right?"

"We all live in Lake Worth, Arizona. The Coalition office was the first to open," Jamie informed her. "We each run our own team. I specialize in missing persons. Cody was a homicide detective when he worked with the regular police force, so he specializes in shifter murders. Zak is a master at undercover work."

Melissa caught up to Trent and ran her fingers through his fur. "And Luca? Cole?"

"Luca was with the ATF and he helps out on all the teams. Cole just took over as an Alpha of his own Pack and heads up the threat rings for the agency. We're not as isolated as the shifters here, but we've made our own family."

"So." Melissa tightened her fingers. "Your mate is human."

Jamie chuckled again. "I was wondering if you'd ask. Brandy is wonderful. She's a librarian and an author. She's sweet while feisty at the same time."

"Did she know you were a shifter when you met?"

"No," Jamie said. "I used to go into the library every week but didn't think someone like her would even give me the time of day. I'd been on my own for so long that my only friends were Cody and Zak. I didn't trust people, especially humans. It was in the early days of forming the Coalition and we weren't well accepted."

She patted Trent's back. "Seems like there's still a lot of that."

Trent nuzzled her hand before he jogged away after picking up the faint trace of someone. Melissa and Jamie continued to talk behind him. Luca was sniffing around east of him through some bushes.

"It is getting better," Jamie said. "It might not feel like it, but most people don't care if we can transform into animals or not. They have their own concerns and lives."

"I hope you're right," Melissa said.

Luca made a quiet yip.

"He's got something," Jamie whispered.

Trent jogged over to Luca's side. As he got closer, he could still pick up the weak scent he'd been trying to follow. Hidden under a straggly shrub was a black backpack, half buried.

"Well, what do we have here?" Jamie murmured. Trent moved over so Jamie could pick up the bag. It appeared the backpack had been abandoned for some time. Trent was having a hard time even catching an old hint of smell.

"Is it one of the shifters? Maybe clothes for when they shift?" Melissa asked. "Magnus told me that was normal."

Jamie pulled out a pair of latex gloves from his back pocket and pulled them on. As he unzipped the backpack, Luca walked behind him and looked out as a guard. Trent lifted his head to peer in the other direction.

"This isn't a shifter's," Jamie said.

Trent looked over.

"Flashlight, map of the area, a knife, and, oh…. What's this?" He pulled out a photo.

"Jesus!" Melissa exclaimed. "That's Annabelle."

Trent snarled. He'd always known whoever was responsible for everything had happened in Brookside had been fixated on Annabelle. The attacks on her, the bar being targeted time and again…

"Why do they have a picture of Annabelle?" Melissa asked. "What's this about?"

"I think while Bustillos is out for the money, Grant has a more personal agenda," Jamie said.

"We know," Melissa said. "He hated shifters."

"But there's something about Annabelle that's making him target her."

"We need to warn the others."

Oh, Trent agreed with that.

"She's with Zak and Logan. She should be safe," Jamie said. He pulled out his cell phone and started to type a message.

"I remember Annabelle saying Grant gave her the creeps," Melissa said. She stepped over to Trent. He leaned against Melissa, letting his body heat comfort her. "I should have followed my instincts and pressed her about it."

"All right. I've given everyone a heads-up. Zak will keep a close eye on Annabelle," Jamie said. "Can either of you get a direction?"

Trent shook his head.

Jamie grunted.

"It does look like the bag's been here a while," Melissa stated. "Which bothers me. How long have they been watching?"

"Too long," Jamie replied. Trent agreed.

"I guess we'll have to continue searching.," Melissa slapped Trent's rump.

He whirled around and made a whoop sound at her.

"Oops." She laughed. "You probably don't like that, do you?"

He was going to torture her when he was human again. Slow, sweet, sensual torture.

"Let's get going," Jamie ordered. He lifted the pack before swinging it over his shoulder.

Trent took off again, this time not only concentrating on strong odors, but looking for any trace of humans. Ever.

It wasn't easy to distinguish the wide variety of smells or determine how old they were. In movies or books, a shifter could always find that shadow or whiff of whoever they were tracking. But this was real life and Trent didn't think the humans were in the forest hiding. After what had taken place the previous evening, they had to be all in or else the entire plan would come apart. Bustillos and Grant had to know the shifters knew what they were up against.

He kept going west, which would take them farther into the state park. They were dangerously close to

Grant's turf. Except while Grant might know the territory, he didn't have a connection to the grass or trees or the animals who roamed. It was the shifters who belonged naturally in the area. Trent could use that to his advantage.

Trent paused. *That's it.* He needed to use his connection to the land to figure out where the humans had come from, which might lead him to where they were going.

Luca bumped his side. He had no way to tell the others what he was thinking. He could shift, tell them, and transform back, but that took too much energy. Multiple shifts would require Trent to eat and refuel. He couldn't chance stumbling across the humans and being too weak to fight.

He hoped the others would just trust him.

Trent used his vision instead of his nose. There was a reason experienced hikers and shifters stayed on marked trails—in order to not disturb the foliage growing, it was important not to trample the ground. Now that he wasn't spending so much power on trying to pick up scents that weren't there, he used his eyes.

There were broken leaves, branches and trampled grass. He raced forward when he spotted the print of a boot. He knew, fuck yes, he was certain that it matched what park rangers wore. He'd seen them many times in the years he'd lived in Brookside. Part of his job was mopping up dirt and mud from the bar floor. He paid attention to details like that. Before Grant had started, there'd been an older ranger who used to visit the bar. He'd been human and this had been before shifters had gone public, so Trent didn't know how the ranger would have felt about them. Still, Trent had always gotten a good vibe from the man, even if he did have a bad habit of tracking mud into the bar.

He nosed the spot for Luca.

"I think Trent found something," Melissa called to Jamie.

"Let him follow it," Jamie advised.

Trent took off again. He glanced over his shoulder. Luca was staying with him. Jamie waved him on.

"Go! I'll watch over Melissa and text our location and what directions we're going to Cody. I won't let you get too far ahead."

Now that Trent had decided to follow this lead, excitement coursed through him. The pattern was easy to spot. Someone had spent a lot of time going back and forth on this unmarked course. Up ahead, there were two directions that were possible. And one was right back to the bar.

He stopped, panting, as he waited for Jamie and Melissa to catch up. Moving his head in the direction of the bar, he tried to signal to Luca what he thought. Luca followed his movement before bobbing his head.

"There you are!" Melissa sprinted toward him.

Trent rested his chin against her arm when she dropped down.

"I told you they'd be fine," Jamie said. He wasn't even out of breath.

Trent considered shifting again. Instead Luca jumped up, placing his paws on Jamie's shoulder.

"What's he doing?" Melissa asked.

"Trying to tell me something," Jamie answered. He never took his attention from Luca, though. "We've been working on non-verbal communication while in our shifter forms. It takes too much out of us to transform, so the teams are working on signaling. He's telling me he needs to run off somewhere, in a hurry."

"Where to?" Melissa questioned.

Luca dropped down and swung his head in the direction Trent wanted to race to.

"That way." Jamie pointed.

"The bar? That's how we'd get back to the bar," Melissa said. There was panic in her voice.

"Go!" Jamie ordered. "I'm calling them at the bar so they know to watch out. We'll meet you there."

Trent didn't need to hear any more. He took off to save his friends.

Melissa had to give it to the shifters. They could move. Trent and Luca were long gone and even though Jamie had slowed down for her, Melissa was barely able to keep running. Jamie wasn't showing any strain. He was even talking to Carter on the phone.

The bar was on high alert. Trent was on the way. Annabelle wasn't even close to the place. If the humans did attack, they wouldn't get away with anything. The trap was set.

"Here," Jamie said. "We'll be able to keep an eye on the back door from this position."

Melissa dropped down behind a tree. Carl was supposed to have the front covered. All the cameras were working and Carter had put better security on his system. As she struggled to catch her breath, Jamie was texting. He had the screen light off, but somehow he still managed. She wouldn't have been able to see the words on the screen.

"Cody is circling above," Jamie whispered.

It must be nice having a bird shifter in the ranks. Cody was able to get a good view of them.

"If you hear three screeches, that means drop down and cover your head," Jamie advised. "That's our code for 'the shit is about to hit the fan'."

Melissa nodded. It had been a good idea for Logan to call in his friends. They were used to working together and knew how to function as part of a team. She was a little bit in awe. If Mac's group performed even half as well as the Coalition had shown, there was a real chance that no one on their side was going to get hurt.

Her pulse slowed, letting Melissa regain her composure. She needed to be alert in case anything happened.

One long bird call came from above.

"There's movement," Jamie murmured. He leaned closer to where she sat. "Don't move."

"Where's Trent? And Luca?" she asked.

"Close," Jamie assured her. "They can move faster than we can."

She pressed her lips together so she wouldn't bombard him with more questions. It wasn't the time or place. She could feel the tension in the air. Something big was going to happen.

"Stay calm," Jamie whispered.

She nodded. Okay, she felt for her weapon, which was on her waist. Melissa pulled it from the holster. She felt better having it in her hand. She didn't have teeth or claws to fight with, but neither did the humans. She was a deputy sheriff. If there was a way to arrest these people, she was going to make sure they spent as much time in jail as possible. Logan had already stated that the humans would face federal charges. This was a federal case since the Coalition was involved. Targeting the shifter community like this was considered a hate crime.

Another long bird cry.

"Get ready," Jamie warned softly.

Melissa tightened her grip on her weapon. From her hiding place, she could see from the corner of the building to the back door. The picnic table Trent had told Melissa he spent a lot of time at was empty. From there, the plan would unfold.

The back door of the bar opened and Calvin stepped out. He had a cigarette lit before the door had slammed closed behind him. Calvin took a long drag before blowing it out. He sighed then strode to the picnic table. Good acting skills. Melissa was watching and she still couldn't detect that Calvin was aware of being watched.

Calvin sat on the table top then peered out into the darkness. There was a good chance he could see them from that distance. She was tempted to wave.

She caught the movement from around the corner right after Jamie had tensed. Two men had their backs to the wall as they slowly crept closer to Calvin. Melissa sucked in her breath as she waited. Jamie leaned forward.

Damn! She grabbed Jamie's arm and pointed. From around the back of the bar, two more figures were approaching to surround Calvin.

Jamie held up his palm to stop her from speaking.

She knew, even as the humans sought out Calvin, the humans themselves were being corralled. How many humans were there? There had to be more than just four. Of course, she couldn't see the other side of the building or even the front.

Calvin tossed the butt of his cigarette out onto the dirt. He rose then stretched.

"Don't move, you filthy creature." One of the men stepped away from the wall and pointed a gun at Calvin.

Calvin jerked then spun around. "Hey! Calm down." He held up his palms, showing he wasn't holding a weapon.

"If you even twitch, I'll shoot you." The guy waved his weapon.

"No, man!" Calvin drawled. "I'm not moving."

"You're going to let us into the bar," the man said. "Just nice and easy."

"No," Calvin responded. "I won't. I won't let you hurt my friends."

The guy stomped toward Calvin. "You'll do what you're told, or I'll kill you right here. I know your friend is watching through the cameras. Stop wasting time."

"What? You couldn't hack into the security system this time?" Calvin taunted.

No! What's he doing? He shouldn't be egging on the bad guys! Melissa wanted to scream and shout at him, but Jamie grabbed her arm, stopping her from rushing forward. She would have ruined everything.

"No, we couldn't," the guy responded. "But it doesn't matter. You're going to take us inside, or I'll shoot you dead before getting inside myself."

"And if I let you in?" Calvin asked.

"I'll leave you and your mate alone. You can ride off on those big bikes of yours and disappear."

"You'll let us go? Me and my mate?" Calvin asked.

"Yes. As long as you promise to never return."

Calvin glanced around, maybe pretending he was just then seeing he was surrounded. He looked scared. Good acting, was Melissa's opinion. "You swear? You'll let me and Duffy go?"

"Just open the door."

"Fine." Calvin nodded. He took a step forward then another. "Don't hurt Duffy."

The guy followed behind Calvin, keeping the gun pointed at him. The other humans closed ranks around them.

"Wait," Jamie cautioned. "Let them get inside. We'll have better control of the situation and cut off any human retreat or backup."

Damn, if she was having a hard time letting things play out, Trent must be going near insane.

Calvin held up a key before he motioned to the door. The human who had been threatening him gave him a hard shove.

"Just open it."

"I don't see Grant," she whispered.

"Okay, good to know." Jamie texted another message.

The humans disappeared into the bar with Calvin.

"Let's make our way closer," Jamie said. "Stay hidden until I give the signal."

"Sure." She crept closer.

Jamie's phone vibrated. "Go!"

Melissa pushed off the ground and ran to the back door. From several yards away, two forms burst out of the tree line—Luca and Trent were backing her up. Melissa dug into her pocket for Trent's key which he'd handed her earlier. She yanked it out as she reached the door.

As quickly as she could, Melissa unlocked the door to hold it open for the two shifters. Trent was through first with Luca at his heels. Jamie brought up the rear. There were no lights, sound or activity. Trent and Luca both walked into the kitchen.

"Hang on to me," Jamie whispered. "I'll lead you through the dark."

Melissa grasped the back of Jamie's shirt. That way they could both still move and defend themselves at the same time.

Trent vanished from the kitchen, heading toward the main bar.

There was a crash and she couldn't hold in a gasp.

"It's okay," Jamie murmured. "Hang on."

Jamie hurried tugging her along. There were more sounds of a fight. She pushed Jamie. "Go! Help!"

She could find her way, but Jamie needed to help their friends. He glanced over his shoulder and nodded. When he let out a fierce roar, the walls actually shook.

Melissa placed her hand on the wall to help guide her.

It looked like the front door was smashed open. She still had her weapon in her hand.

The yips, cries and shouts were so loud.

She remembered another hall with the sound of a fight. She'd taken a life, and now the same people were trying to tear away her new family. Melissa took a deep breath and, relying on her instincts, dashed in the direction of the battle.

"Stop."

Melissa skidded to a halt as a knife was thrust her in her direction. Grant stepped out of the shadows.

She frowned, not understanding. *What the hell?* Was Grant letting his friends confront the shifters without him?

"Hand me your weapon," Grant ordered.

"No." Melissa wasn't stupid. If she gave up her gun, Grant would kill her.

"It's not you I'm after," Grant told her. "You're human."

"You're looking for Annabelle," she guessed.

"Tell me where she is and I'll let you go."

"Not going to happen," Melissa responded.

Grant lunged at her. She tried to get her hand up and fire, but she didn't think she hit him. He knocked her off her feet, but she still held on to her weapon. *Thank God for training.* Melissa rolled and came up on her knees.

Grant punched her. Hard.

Melissa fell back.

His foot came down on her wrist and she screamed as he stomped. She could no longer hang on to the gun.

"Now," Grant said. He gripped her hair and yanked her up. "Where is she?"

"Nowhere close to here." Melissa didn't know if that was true or not. For all she knew, the teams had made it back and were kicking the humans' asses.

"I know," Grant snapped. "That's why I didn't just kill you."

She didn't have time to get her feet under her as he started to drag her toward the back door.

"No!" She clawed at his wrist.

Grant dropped her long enough to kick her several times in the ribs. Each blow felt like a knife stabbing into her. She could barely breathe. Melissa coughed and gasped. He gripped the collar of her shirt, hauling her again.

She couldn't lift herself up enough to go after his hand again. Instead she dug her nails into his leg. Melissa couldn't let him get her outside. And there was no way she'd take him to Annabelle. Grant had some kind of unnatural obsession with her.

"Stop fighting," Grant said as she struggled. "I swear you bitches are more trouble than you're worth."

They were halfway through the kitchen now.

Melissa kicked out, connecting with his knee. Grant grunted. He fell on her. Grant recovered before she could. He hit her again. Melissa tasted blood and spat it into his face.

"I'm going to enjoy killing you," he told her.

"Not if I kill you first." She scratched and bit, using every bit of fight she had inside her.

A low, loud growl echoed around the kitchen.

Melissa stopped grappling with Grant. He wrapped his arm around her throat and wrenched her back against him.

The kitchen light flicked on. Grant yelled. A pair of goggles dropped into her lap. Well, that explained why he'd been able to see better than her.

"Let her go." Logan stepped closer. He must had been the one to turn on the lights. Trent was crouched down, snarling, with one side of his lip lifted.

"No!" she cried. "He wants Annabelle."

Trent rumbled out his displeasure.

"Annabelle is safe," Logan said. "All your buddies are either dead or in cuffs, Grant. Give up now."

"Never," Grant spat. "And if you come any closer, I'll snap her neck."

Melissa really didn't want to have her neck snapped. She looked at Trent. His rage shone in the brightness of the intelligent eyes staring back at her. He would protect her. That was the one promise he'd made.

She trusted he would keep the promise.

"You're going to let her go and put your hands up or I'm going to let Trent rip out your throat," Logan stated.

"No," Grant said. "I'm going to walk out of here and I'll be taking her with me."

"If you try to take her out of here, you wouldn't make it two steps." Logan gestured to Trent. "Do you think he'll let you take her?"

"Then bring me back the other one," Grant demanded. "The one responsible for my brother's death."

"There is no one here who had anything to do with Jesus' death," Logan said.

"It was her! I recognize her," Grant yelled.

"You're wrong," Logan told him. "I've read the report. The two shifters your brother tried to kill that night have never been here."

"Lies!" Grant screamed. He flexed his arm, which began to cut off her oxygen. "My brother was hunting. Just like he always did that time of year. They lied and said he attacked two people. People? You're all animals. You can kill but we can't!"

Melissa tried to get Grant's arm to loosen. She dug her nails into his forearm as hard as she could. He didn't respond, though. He was lost in whatever crazy scheme was going on in his mind. *He* was crazy.

"Listen to me, Grant," Logan spoke quietly. "Your brother shot at two shifters who had been enjoying a run in their animal form. The male transformed and tried to talk to Jesus. Your brother still tried to kill him and the man defended himself."

"No! That animal killed my brother."

Melissa started to see spots.

"Release her," Logan demanded.

"I want to see the other one!" Grant ordered.

"I'm here," Annabelle said as she stepped into the kitchen with her arms raised.

The pressure against Melissa's throat eased and she sucked in air as fast as she could.

"Let my friend go," Annabelle pleaded. "Melissa doesn't have anything to do with this."

"Come closer," Grant commanded.

"Stay back, Annabelle," Logan said.

"It's me he wants," Annabelle argued. She turned to Melissa. "It's going to be okay, Melissa. He's not going to hurt you."

"Closer," Grant repeated.

Annabelle shuffled forward.

"Get back," Melissa rasped. She did not want Annabelle hurt.

"I'll be fine," Annabelle said. "I have to apologize to Grant."

"Yes, you do." Grant rose, bringing Melissa up with him.

"So let her go and take me instead," Annabelle offered.

"No!" Melissa and Logan said at the same time.

Annabelle was so brave facing off against a crazed man who wanted to kill her. Grant's hold on Melissa was practically nonexistent now. She could break it. Grant was staring at Annabelle with a gleam in his eyes.

When Annabelle passed Logan, he tried to reach out to her, but she slipped away.

Grant's entire attention was on Annabelle.

Melissa pulled free, but Grant didn't seem to notice. She whirled around and slammed her fist into his throat.

"Fuck!" Grant dropped down holding his throat.

Trent lunged, landing on top of Grant. Logan and Annabelle grabbed Melissa, pulling her out of harm's way. There was a growl then a cry.

"I got him," Mac said as he strode forward with a pair of cuffs.

Melissa was having a hard time staying focused on what Annabelle was saying to her. Her entire body ached, but it was her head that pounded.

"Baby." Trent's hands were cool against her cheek. "Look at me."

She blinked. Melissa had closed her eyes at some point.

"We're going to get you some medical attention," Trent said.

"Annabelle," she managed.

"She's fine," Trent assured her. "It's over. Everyone is in custody."

"It's over," she repeated. She needed to hear those words again.

"Yes, it's over. We even have Ramon Bustillos. He was parked in town and Magnus caught him," Trent said.

"Oh." Her legs gave out, but he caught her up against his chest.

"Just relax and let me hold me," he whispered.

"I think I need a shower," she said. "I feel dirty."

"I will scrub every inch of you before I lay you down and love every inch I cleaned."

That sounded like heaven to her.

Chapter Eleven

Trent passed Jamie and Zak bottles of beer before he slipped his arm around Melissa's shoulder. She cuddled closer to him as if that was the most natural thing in the world. Trent loved the affection.

It'd only been two days since they'd taken down Bustillos, Grant and the other humans, but things couldn't be better. Trent could peer around the yard and see that even though there would always be threats and people out to hurt shifters, they'd managed to keep everyone in Brookside safe. Mac's group and the sheriff's department were always going to be there. And they had friends. Powerful friends who came with one phone call.

Most of the Brookside residents were attending the large thank-you barbecue for the Lake Worth Coalition agents. Everyone was thankful for the securing of their town. Things could now go back to normal.

"This is quite the turnout," Melissa stated.

"I noticed that several people have greeted you," Trent said. "It appears you've become quite popular."

She smiled. At first, Melissa had seemed shocked that anyone would talk to her. It had started with Mr. Pritcher, then more of the residents. Having Melissa help keep the town safe had allowed the townsfolk to see she'd go out of her way to protect them. Trent liked her being so happy. Bruises still covered her face and stomach, but she was moving around much better. Trent was still struggling with the nightmares from seeing her with Grant's arm around her neck. With her being human, Melissa was more vulnerable than him and the shifters.

"I have to admit I prefer the smiles to the cold shoulder," she confessed.

"I like it here," Jamie said. "I promised Brandy I'd bring her as soon as we got some time away. She loves the idea of an entire town of shifters."

"I'd like to meet her," Melissa said.

"I think you all should bring your mates," Trent offered. "A little break from the city when you need it."

Zak lifted his beer. "I'm all for that. Abilene is going to love Annabelle."

Trent glanced over to the tree Annabelle had escaped to. She still had a hard time around a lot of people. Logan was leaning back against the tree trunk laughing with Luca and Fredrick.

Their little family was growing and Trent was okay with that.

He kissed the side of Melissa's head. If she hadn't shown up in his town, he wouldn't be thinking about the future like he was now. The program that Mac ran was important and they did good work, but they needed to do more to help shifters.

"Speaking of my mate," Zak said as his phone rang. "That's her."

Jamie grinned. "Tell her I said hi."

Zak nodded before strolling away with his phone in his hand.

"Abilene has been such a good influence on him," Jamie said. "I was pretty sure we were going to lose him to the dark side before he met her." He eyed Trent. "Sometimes what happens in the past can keep us from realizing what's right in front of us."

Trent nodded at the words directed to him. "Other times our past is what we need to face in order to move forward."

"I'm glad you said that," Jamie responded. "I asked Cody to look into your partner's death when you were with the LAPD."

"What?" Trent couldn't help but tense.

Melissa grasped the back of his shirt. "Why would you do that?"

Jamie glanced from her to him. "The LAPD is not following the directions of federal agencies or laws in place. The top brass is being replaced even as we speak, but we need to take down the ones on the streets. The LAPD has the highest number of complaints and in-house death of shifters."

"That's a big order to fill," Melissa stated.

"Which is why we need the two of you," Jamie said.

"I won't go back," Trent declared. This was his home, his family now. As much as he wanted to make a difference, he needed to stay surrounded by his family.

"I wouldn't expect you to," Jamie said. "But we need your help, anyway. We're sending a team from the Coalition there."

"What would we have to do?" Melissa asked.

Of course, she would want to help. She'd spent years trying to right every wrong the LAPD had done to shifters.

"Names, dates and cases that our agents need to be aware of," Jamie answered. "There might be more that the field agents need, but that information would help get us started."

Trent turned to Melissa.

"It's up to you," she said. "I'm here now and I'm not leaving."

He nodded. "I can tell you about what I experienced before I left."

"Great." Jamie slapped him on the back. "I'm going to grab a burger."

"I'll talk to you later," Trent told him.

As Jamie walked away, Melissa slipped in front of Trent, putting both arms around his waist. "You sure you want to get involved with the LAPD? I can give the Coalition the information they need and keep you out of everything."

"No." Trent shook his head. "I want to do it together. I already let you take the brunt of what should have been my fight. I won't leave you like that again."

She grinned. "I like the sound of that."

He carded his fingers through her hair. "I promised you that I'd always protect you. Especially against the assholes who I really want to track down and shove my boot up their ass."

Melissa laughed. "I love you."

Trent turned Melissa so she was facing their friends with her back to his chest. "Look at all these people who needed us to stop someone from taking everything from them. We did that. And it's only the beginning. We'll help."

Her weight felt good against him. Trent rested his chin on the top of her head. Cody had shifted and was perched on a branch not too far from where Annabelle was sitting. She was swiping at him, but by the way her tail was wagging, she was enjoying Cody's evasive moves. Jamie was indeed stuffing his face with food beside Mac, Zak, Luca and Magnus.

The sun shone above and it felt good to no longer be hiding away.

"Come on." Melissa tugged him toward the bar.

"Where are we going?" Trent followed behind her, though. If Melissa wanted some time alone, he was more than willing. Hell, it was a better idea then hanging out with a bunch of men, even if they were his friends. That didn't mean he wouldn't tease her. "I haven't eaten yet."

"You'll get fed," she said. "I promise."

Trent let Melissa lead them back to his room. They'd eventually need to decide if they'd stay at her house or in The Den. Trent wasn't sure which he preferred. While he liked the privacy of her house, he also needed to be around the others. He'd bring it up later. At the moment, he was just happy to go to bed with her each night and wake up with her every morning.

She paused outside his door. "I thought that we could start dividing our time between your place and mine. You need to be here on the weekends, so maybe midweek we can go back to my house."

Guess our thoughts were on the same lines. "That's perfect."

"Now," she said, pushing the door open. "I want some time alone with you."

Trent grinned. He'd spent all night loving her and she couldn't get enough. That was a stroke to his ego. "We have a yard full of people."

"I don't care," Melissa said. "I feel like I need to make up for lost time."

"We have the rest of our lives, but I will never turn you down." He picked her up to carry her to the bed.

He set her down and she knelt on the mattress before reaching for him. Melissa ran her palms along his stomach, tugging his T-shirt up.

Trent leaned down and kissed her. He slipped his tongue inside her mouth, relishing her unique flavor. He was already moaning as he pushed her back and covered her body with his.

"So good," she murmured against his lips. "Show me again how good we are together."

"I will," Trent promised. "This is only the beginning."

Want to see more from this author? Here's a taster for you to enjoy!

Bloodlines
Crissy Smith

Excerpt

Kieran Smith hissed as the needle was pulled out of his arm.

"Don't be a baby," Dean Westbridge taunted without sympathy. He slapped a Band-Aid onto Kieran's wound with a smirk.

He growled at Dean, but his heart wasn't really in the threat. Six weeks after Kieran had found out that there might be something wrong with him, there were still no answers. He needed Dean in order to figure this shit out. The doctor who had tortured and experimented on him for ten years let it out that he'd added unknown concoctions to Kieran's DNA. Sure, Kieran had realized that he was stronger and faster than other Walkers, but he'd attributed it to his advanced agent training. Now, it turned out that he was an even bigger freak than he'd first thought.

"How're you feeling? Have you noticed anything out of the ordinary?" Dean questioned.

Kieran wished he could say for sure. Being a Day Walker already made him different from other paranormals since there were very few of his kind. There weren't many others he knew to compare himself to. The Walkers that he did know didn't exactly like to talk about their abilities. In response to Dean's question, he shrugged.

Dean sighed. "I need you to tell me what's going on."

"I realize that," Kieran said. "I don't know the answer."

The human agent walked across the room to set the vials of blood he'd taken from Kieran and placed them in a bag. Kieran wouldn't consider Dean a friend but pretty close. Dean had been the partner of Dakota, Kieran's lover, for many years, so that connection held them together. Kieran made an attempt to get along with Dean for Dakota's sake.

"How're things going with Dakota?" Dean asked from the other side of the room.

Kieran stiffened. He couldn't help his reaction. "Why?"

"Jeez, Kieran," Dean complained. "I didn't mean anything by the question. I just wanted to make sure the two of you are okay. There's been a lot going on. You two moved into the new suite, right?"

"Sorry," Kieran muttered. It hadn't been an easy month and a half since they'd taken down the group responsible for the death, torture and kidnapping of both Walkers and shifters. Finding out that the same organization they worked for had high-powered agents involved had thrown them off their game. Trust, something that was hard for Kieran at normal time, was now nonexistent. Only his promise to Dakota had him coming to see Dean every week. If it wasn't for his lover's concern, Kieran would be staying far away from anyone who wasn't part of his inner circle.

"The new place is bigger, so Dakota likes it. I enjoy staying at the hotel to remain close to Alex. I guess it's just weird buying a suite with Dakota. Like I'm waiting for her to get tired of my bullshit and take off." His honesty surprised him. Kieran never talked about his feelings. Especially not with someone like Dean, who he didn't know all that well. He moaned. "Forget I said anything, please."

"Look, man," Dean said, "Dakota loves you. If you want to talk to me, I'm more than happy to listen. I want to help figure out what's going on for the both of you. Just give me time."

In response to Dean's words, Kieran nodded. It wasn't easy for him to rely on anyone except himself. He still held himself back from Remy, his wolf shifter partner, who he'd worked with since joining the Organization. He yanked down the sleeve of his black sweater before standing. He appreciated Dean letting him come down to his lab instead of him having to go into the medical wing. Kieran's past with medical experiments was only one of the many issues that he had to try to deal with. If he hadn't had the control of someone much older than he actually was, Kieran could have ended up being a danger to those around him.

Everyone around him was aware of the very thin line that Kieran walked.

Even his partner and lover knew that at any time, Kieran could fall off the straight and narrow. They loved him, anyway.

If it wasn't for the support of the small collection of friends, his family now, Kieran probably would have gone to the dark side years ago. But, luckily for the world, Kieran had motivation to remain sane and honest.

"Okay," Dean announced, drawing Kieran from his thoughts. "I'll send these off and see if there've been any changes."

"Thanks." Kieran shoved his hands into the pockets of his dark-washed jeans before strolling toward the door.

"Hey, K!"

Kieran paused, although he didn't turn.

"You're going to be okay. I'm going to make certain."

Without another word, Kieran left Dean's lab. He wasn't on shift tonight and he hated having time off. Now, he'd spend the evening thinking about Dean and his damn tests. Dean couldn't and shouldn't make promises that might be impossible to keep. Kieran needed a distraction. One of his favorite activities was messing with the other agents around, but, since he'd seen his boss's vehicle outside earlier, he knew better.

Caspar might give him more leeway than anyone else, but Kieran knew when not to press his luck. Having to deal with the higher-ups of the Organization as well as the Shifter Coalition running their own investigation was leading to Caspar being in a very bad mood. While Kieran might have liked to have taken his boss's mind off everything going on and provide some entertainment, he'd promised Dakota that he'd behave.

He was just about to reach the elevator when his cell rang. Kieran pulled the black device from his pocket and read the screen. Lettie, his former co-worker from his previous post, was calling. He still spoke to her when she decided he needed to know something, so she wouldn't be calling for no reason.

"What's up?" he asked in greeting.

"Your girl just called in for backup," Lettie said. "I don't like what I'm hearing."

Kieran stiffened. Lettie was the best fucking hacker in the world. He didn't know why she continued to monitor them even when she'd been assigned to a different office, but he was grateful. "Where is she?" he demanded.

"3412 North Washington, behind a closed electronic store. The original call was for a reported sighting of a wild animal. Wolf maybe," Lettie answered.

"And?" Kieran pressed. Dakota could handle a wolf shifter with no problem. A jaguar shifter, she was powerful, fast and smart. She was also highly trained.

"Neighbors are calling in more animal sounds and when Dakota radioed for backup, she was cut off," Lettie explained.

He didn't need to hear any more. Kieran went to the stairwell exit instead of waiting for the elevator. He ran down the steps two at a time. "Got it." He hung up, needing to concentrate on getting to his lover. There were times when he hated what she did for a living. But, unlike him, Dakota wouldn't ever be able to leave the Organization.

Centuries ago, a small group of Walkers, shifters and humans had decided to form an agency that would work in the shadows to keep the innocent and unaware humans from discovering the paranormal world. The entire Organization was staffed from the bloodlines of the original group. Because Dakota had been born the first child of a family involved, she'd been commissioned to service. She hadn't been given a choice. From a young age, she'd been aware that she wouldn't be raised or loved by her family. She only had one purpose — to become an agent.

As far as Kieran knew, he was the only active agent who didn't stem from the original families. Caspar had brought him in after Kieran had been rescued. Kieran often wondered why Caspar had enfolded him into the world of the Organization, but it didn't really matter. Kieran was an agent and he could make a choice to leave if he wanted. He wouldn't, though. There was no way he'd leave his partner or lover behind. He was in for life, because Dakota and Remy were. There was no retirement for Organization agents. They either died in the line of service or were employed until their usefulness ran out.

He slammed through the last barrier opening up into the underground parking lot then raced through the night toward his bike, intent on getting to Dakota. As was his habit, he'd parked his Harley down the street instead of in front of the building that housed their offices.

Kieran didn't bother with a helmet. He merely got his bike started and roared off. The area that Dakota had called from was across town. As she'd called for backup, another agent should be closer than him, but he didn't trust anyone else to have her back. She worked with a bear shifter and human, but Kieran was a Walker. The abilities and power that he offered was unmatched by any other agent. He was the only Walker in the Las Vegas division.

Swerving in and out of traffic, Kieran sped toward Dakota.

It was a good thing that he didn't have to be worried about being killed in an accident with the chances he took. The heavy Vegas traffic was always a hardship to get through, but at nine at night on a Friday, it was damn near impossible. This was the exact reason he rode his bike. He was able to fit through spaces and, yes, he might have used a couple of sidewalks, as well.

Flashing lights, chaos and screaming greeted him when he pulled into the parking lot of a boarded-up bar. He skidded his motorcycle to a stop, ignoring the human police officers trying to wave him away. It was obvious to Kieran that the humans would be no help in this situation.

"Sir! Get back on your bike and leave the area!" a young, freckled faced officer ordered.

Kieran had the urge to flash his fangs at the damn kid. Hell, he couldn't be older than twenty-one. This little twerp was absolutely no competition to Kieran. He resisted scaring the crap out of the officer. "I'm with her." He pointed toward Dakota.

"Oh, sure," the officer replied, paling a little.

Kieran held back a smirk. The young policeman no doubt thought he was some sort of shifter. But while the shifters of the world had come out to the public several years ago, letting their existence be known, Walkers were still kept secret. There was enough drama with humans knowing about shifters. Vampires, or whatever they wanted to name his species, would have the humans in a massive panic.

He stalked with care toward where Dakota was crouched peering in a hole inside the bar. Her two partners, Gabe and Dare, stood at her back, watching the crowds. While Dakota's attention was on whatever was happening inside, they had her six. Kieran approved.

"What's going on?" he asked, joining them.

"We think there's an injured shifter inside," Dare told him. "And a wolf and coyote shifter won't let us get close enough to get a good look, though."

Fuck, an injured shifter can cause a lot of damage if they panic.

"It's okay," Dakota was murmuring. "I know you're scared, but we're not here to hurt you."

She'd used that tone with him when Kieran was coming out of a nightmare or an episode of his past. He'd always found it comforting. Kieran hoped whoever she was speaking to picked up the honesty in her tone.

Kieran dropped to his knees behind her. "What do you need?" he whispered. He needed to stay out sight for now. If the shifters saw him, they'd pick up on his power and things could get a lot worse.

Dakota turned her head. "You're supposed to be off tonight."

He shrugged. There was no reason for her to be aware that Lettie monitored her calls when she was on duty. "I was in the neighborhood."

She scoffed. "I bet. We'll discuss this later. I sent the other agents to see if there was any other way inside. I don't want to force our way in if we can help it."

Yeah, the possible bloodshed involved wasn't good. Especially with humans close by.

"Just three inside?" he asked.

"That's all I can smell." She leaned back. "It's weird — they're really young. And how often do you see three different species together?"

"They've all shifted?"

"They are now. When we got here, just the bobcat and wolf were, but now the coyote has, as well. That's probably how they feel the safest."

"Sorry, Dakota." Two agents came from around the side of the building. "It's boarded up good. There's no way to get inside without ripping off some of the wood."

She shook her head. "That'd make too much noise. Send them into a panic."

"What do you want to do?" Kieran inquired. He could already tell that she was coming up with a plan.

"I can shift and go in."

"No." There was no question. He was not going to allow her to put herself in danger that way.

"K," she murmured. "We have to do this quick. There's no telling when a damn news crew will show up. I don't want these kids to be on camera. We need to get them out of here."

He glanced around and knew she was right. For the last several months, it had seemed that someone was tipping off reporters to every incident that they were investigating. That wasn't good when their Organization was meant to work in secret. Luckily, the news had associated them with the Shifter Coalition instead of realizing they were something much more dangerous. Already, a ton of people stood at the taped-off area where the local PD was holding them back. Numerous cell phones were being pointed at them as the humans took pictures and videos. He growled, still hating technology. When he'd first started working for the Organization, things had been so much simpler. He'd not had to worry about someone catching him and exposing his secrets. Now, the lives of the agents were put in jeopardy every time someone showed up to get their fifteen minutes of fame.

"I can go around the back and just punch my way inside," he said. "No one will even see me." Kieran would rather put himself in danger than her. What he was couldn't get out. The world was still stressing over the existence of shifters. If humans learned of vampire-type creatures, there'd be no peace for the paranormal community.

"Can't," Dakota said. "Caspar would kick both our asses if someone captured that."

He grunted. Like he gave a damn about what Caspar thought if it meant keeping Dakota safe. The more screen time she received, the less chance she'd be able to do her job. Dakota actually loved being with the Organization and protecting innocents while Kieran just didn't like to be bored. He found the excitement and danger worth the time he put in for work. Kieran wasn't a good person. He'd come to terms with his faults a long time ago. Dakota made him want to be a better man, but Kieran wasn't even sure that was possible.

"I'll shift. In my jaguar form, they should be more willing to follow me. I'm more dominant and their instincts will be to cower. I can handle this."

"Or they'll attack as soon as you get inside," he argued. "It'll be three against one."

"They're only kids, K."

God damn it, he didn't want her going in there alone, where he couldn't see or help. He also wasn't happy about her having to reveal her animal side in front of the public. "You." He pointed at one of the agents. "You got an SUV?"

"Yes, sir."

"Back it up to right here," Kieran ordered. "As close as you can get."

"Right away!" The male agent, human, hurried off.

"What are you doing?" Dakota gripped his wrist, frowning.

"You can transform inside. I don't want anyone seeing you. I'll open the back and you can jump from the vehicle to the building. If someone has the right angle, they might catch you, but it's the best we can do."

She nodded. "Good idea." Her features, which had been drawn and tight, softened. When she looked at him like that, Kieran felt like a king. Deep down, he knew eventually she'd stop when he disappointed her. For now, it was enough that she still believed in him.

"I'm staying right by the opening. I swear that if you get hurt, I will not be happy."

"I know." She lifted her hand to cup his cheek. "But remember that they're just scared kids."

He loved her. God, just looking at her concern-filled eyes, he lost his breath. After having had to live her entire life on her own, knowing she had no control about her future, Dakota was still the kindest person he'd ever met. The shifters inside were a threat. Dakota could choose to use force and capture them. Instead, she was revealing herself in order to help them.

She impressed the hell out of him.

It was probably his instincts, as well as past events of his life, which led him to want to use force to end the situation. Not that the kids inside would be harmed, but it'd take less time to force his way in and capture them. That made him feel shitty. Another reminder that he was truly a monster. He'd killed and he'd have to live with that. Sure, he'd only eliminated paranormals who had broken the law and hurt others, but he was tainted. Dakota lived her life for others. It was a small wonder what the hell she was doing with him.

"Be careful," he demanded.

"I always am." She rocked forward to press her lips against his.

Kieran grabbed the back of her head, forcing the quick peck she'd meant into a deep, meaningful kiss. Dakota opened for his probing tongue and her unique flavor burst onto his. He'd claim and mark her in any way that he could.

"The vehicle is coming," Dare said in obvious amusement. "Unless you want to go ahead and undress her here in front of everyone."

Kieran pulled away so he could glare at Dakota's partner. If humans hadn't been around, he would have flashed some fang.

Dare laughed. Kieran liked it better when everyone was terrified of him.

Dakota patted his knee before she stood. He followed suit. As Dakota moved off to the side, Kieran directed the agent in backing up. When the SUV was where he wanted it, Kieran opened the back door for Dakota.

"We're going to discuss you pushing into my call later," she warned him.

"Sure." Kieran would do it again. They both knew that.

"I mean it," she said. "You need a night off."

No, he didn't. Kieran needed to stay busy. The unease and twitchiness he'd always felt was stronger than ever. It was as though he could sense something big was going to happen. And when things happened to Kieran, they were always bad. He hoped all hell wasn't going to break out that night. Kieran was tired— exhausted, really. He could fight but hoped he wouldn't have to. "If I hear anything going wrong, I'll get inside."

With a roll of her eyes, Dakota climbed into the back seat. He slammed the door closed before motioning the other agents where he wanted them. He'd be the one closest to the opening. He wasn't kidding. If he thought she was in danger, he wouldn't care what he had to do to get to Dakota.

Inside the dark vehicle, Dakota was pulling off her shirt. Kieran walked to the back so he'd be able to open the hatch when she was ready.

As he waited, he looked around with a fierce look. A couple of the humans gawking started to shuffle where they stood. He was intimidating and he knew it. Kieran dared anyone to come close.

About the Author

Crissy Smith lives in Texas with her husband, daughter, and three Labrador retrievers. The three dogs love to curl up under her computer desk and nap while she writes. It doesn't leave a lot of room for her but what's a woman to do?

When not writing or reading, she enjoys hunting, camping and shooting. But she has a girly side too and is addicted to pedicures and coffee.

She has been writing since she was a teenager and still loves everything to do with the paranormal. Her stories and characters all have a place in her heart. She loves the Alpha male, the dominant werewolf, and the Master vampire, which find their way in most of her books.

Learn more about the characters she has created at her website where they have their very own page. It will be updated from time to time to let you know what's going on with them. Also you can find out who will be in the next book.

Crissy loves to hear from readers. You can find her contact information, website details and author profile page at http://www.totallybound.com.

TOTALLY
BOUND

Home of Erotic Romance